A Better Offer

Alyssa Evans

Book Cover by Alyssa Evans

Contents

Chapter 1

Kalista pressed her phone to her ear, her silk gown brushing against her legs as she paced the room. The candles flickered softly on the dining table, casting shadows against the glass walls of her penthouse. Her phone buzzed, and when she saw Natalia's name, she sighed but answered.

"This better be quick. Marius is on his way over."

Natalia's voice was tight and hurried. "Kali, check your messages. Right now."

Kalista frowned. "Why? What's going on?"

"Just read them. You need to see it to believe it."

The tension in Natalia's voice made Kalista's stomach churn. Lowering the phone, she swiped to her texts. There it was—an unread message from Alina Pavlos, an acquaintance who ran in the same circles as her and Marius.

Two images.

She tapped open the first photo, and her world tilted.

Marius. Kissing another woman. His hand gripping her waist like it belonged there. In the second photo, his lips pressed along the curve of the woman's neck—an intimate, familiar touch.

Kalista stared at the photos, her pulse roaring in her ears. She felt frozen, suspended between disbelief and the crushing weight of realization.

Natalia's voice filtered back in. "Kali...?"

She forced herself to take a shallow breath. "Thanks, Talia. I'll call you later."

"Kali—"

She ended the call, her thumb hovering for a moment before she hit Call on Marius's contact. The phone barely rang twice before he answered, his voice smooth and casual, like everything was normal.

"Hey, babe. Running a little late—should be there in ten."

"Don't bother."

A beat of silence. Then his voice, still smooth but edged with irritation. "What are you talking about?"

"I know, Marius."

The silence on the other end stretched—just long enough to feel deliberate. Then came a sigh, so dismissive it made her skin prickle.

"Look, Kali...whatever you think you know, it's not what it seems."

Her hand tightened around the phone. "You kissed another woman. I saw the photos."

"Come on," he said, as if she were a child throwing a tantrum. "It wasn't serious. Don't blow this out of proportion."

"Out of proportion?" Her voice sharpened. "We're engaged, Marius."

His sigh was long and patronizing. "Do we really need to do this over the phone?"

"We *really* do."

He clicked his tongue, an exasperated sound. "You're being dramatic, Kali. It didn't mean anything. She's just...someone. You know how these things are."

The sheer arrogance in his tone knocked the air from her lungs. "*No, Marius.* I don't know how these things are."

"Okay, fine." His voice was clipped, as if placating her. "I get it. You're upset. But do you really want to throw away everything we've built over one mistake?"

Kalista swallowed the hot lump rising in her throat, forcing herself to stay calm. "What exactly have we built, Marius? Because from where I'm standing, it looks like nothing."

He sighed, tired now, as if this conversation was a nuisance he didn't have time for. "Look, I'll explain everything when I get there. Just—cool off, okay?"

"No." Her voice was ice. "We're done."

She ended the call before he could respond and tossed the phone onto the counter with more force than necessary.

The engagement ring on her finger burned like a brand. She slid it off, holding it in her palm for a moment before letting it drop onto the table.

The soft clink echoed through the quiet room, a sound that carried all the weight of an ending.

———◆○◆———

Stavros removed his glasses and rubbed the bridge of his nose, as if the weight of the discussion had been building for a while.

"I'll be sixty-three next year," he began. "The board thinks it's time I start pulling back. They want someone younger at the helm."

Kalista leaned back in her chair, crossing her arms. "And that someone is supposed to be me."

Stavros gave a slow nod. "That was always the plan."

Kalista let out a frustrated breath. "You know that wasn't my plan. The idea was for Marius to take over the business side, remember?" She laughed bitterly. "He was supposed to run things, and I'd stay in my lane with the design team."

Her father's expression didn't change, but there was a flicker of something —maybe sympathy, or just recognition—before he responded. "I know that was your idea."

"And obviously, it's going to take some time to...rethink that," she added, her words tight.

Stavros gave her a long, steady look. "Time isn't something the board is willing to give us, Kali. They don't care that Marius didn't work out. They care about stability."

"So marry someone else?" she said dryly. "Is that your solution?"

His lips twitched, but not into a smile. "You know that's not what I'm saying."

Kalista pressed her fingers against her temple. "Dad, you've been telling me for years that I need to step up, but we both know I'm not the person you want running things."

Stavros leaned forward, folding his hands on the table. "I don't want anyone else running things either."

"You just want me to figure out how to be a CEO overnight?"

"No." He met her gaze evenly. "But I want you to try. I want you to start thinking beyond just design. Vorlákis Enterprises needs leadership, and it needs to come from someone who understands the soul of the company."

She shook her head, frustration bubbling to the surface. "I'm not a leader, Dad. I don't even like this part of the business. That's why I had Marius in the first place."

Stavros's expression softened just a fraction. "Marius wasn't the right man for you—or for this company. You're going to have to stop hiding behind that plan, Kali. It didn't work."

The truth in his words hit her like a slap, and for a moment, all she could do was sit in the quiet weight of it.

"What if I don't want this?" she whispered.

"Then the board will push for someone else," Stavros said without hesitation. "An outsider."

Kalista's stomach twisted. There was no need to elaborate on what that would mean. If control of Vorlákis Enterprises left their family, everything her father had built—and everything her grandparents had fought for—would be at risk.

"You might not think you belong in this seat," Stavros continued. "But you're wrong. You have more potential than you realize."

Kalista exhaled sharply through her nose, the weight of his words settling over her. She had always run from this responsibility, but now it was catching up with her. Faster than she could dodge it.

"You really think I can do this?" she asked quietly, almost afraid to hear the answer.

"I do." Stavros's voice was steady, and for once, it didn't sound like an expectation. It sounded like belief. "But you have to decide whether or not you're going to try."

Before she could say anything, the door swung open and his assistant entered, placing a folder on the table.

Before Kalista could respond, the door opened, and one of Stavros's assistants stepped in, carrying a slim black folder.

"We've identified several companies worth watching," the assistant said, placing the folder on the table between them. "A few might be viable for acquisition if their financial situations continue to decline."

Stavros opened the folder and scanned the list, nodding as he flipped through the pages. "Elysium Retail, Corinthian Luxe, and Drakov Holdings...All showing signs of trouble."

Kalista's pulse quickened at the mention of the last name.

"The first two have weak liquidity positions," the assistant continued. "But Drakov Holdings has been sustaining heavy losses for months. If they don't secure new financing soon, they'll be forced to liquidate assets."

Kalista kept her expression neutral, but inside, satisfaction flickered. Marius's empire was crumbling—just like his promises.

Stavros turned another page. "Any signs of competition?"

"Yes," the assistant replied. "Soren Kastellanos has already made inquiries about Drakov Holdings."

Kalista stiffened. Of course Soren was circling. He was always among the first to spot blood in the water. If he acquired Drakov, he wouldn't just salvage it—he'd gut it, rebuild it, and profit immensely in the process.

Her father closed the folder with a decisive snap and gave her a pointed look. "If we want to move on any of these, we'll need to act soon."

But Kalista was barely listening. Her focus had narrowed to one name: *Drakov Holdings.*

This wasn't just business—it was personal.

Her father watched her carefully, clearly aware of the storm brewing beneath her calm exterior. "You know what needs to be done, Kali."

She inhaled deeply, the weight of expectation settling on her chest once again. But this time, the idea of taking action didn't feel quite as suffocating. If she was going to step up, she would do it on her terms—and *her* way.

"I'll think about it," she said, rising from her chair.

Stavros gave her a small nod, his expression measured. "That's all I ask."

The din of polite conversation and the soft clink of champagne flutes filled the grand ballroom, where the city's elite mingled beneath shimmering chandeliers. Kalista moved through the crowd with effortless grace, though her thoughts were far from the glittering world around her.

Her silk gown, a deep sapphire she'd designed herself, clung perfectly to her frame, but tonight, it felt more like armor. She hadn't wanted to come to this gala, but Stavros insisted. "People need to see you," he'd said. "The board needs to see you." And perhaps, she admitted privately, she needed the distraction.

Still, no amount of champagne or polite conversation could dull the frustration simmering beneath her calm exterior. Everywhere she turned, someone else wanted something from her—whether it was praise for her latest collection or some subtle hint at what was next for Vorlákis Enterprises. But no one asked what she wanted.

She was about to slip away to the quieter edge of the room when she spotted him—Soren Kastellanos.

He cut through the crowd like a shark through water, his gaze sharp and deliberate, every movement smooth and purposeful. He wasn't just walking

—he was choosing where to be, when to be there, and whom to speak to. And now, his dark eyes were locked on her.

Before she could decide how to react, he was standing in front of her, his presence magnetic. "Kalista Vorlákis." His voice was low and smooth, carrying just enough intrigue to feel dangerous. "I've been meaning to introduce myself."

She arched an eyebrow, matching his calm energy. "I'd say I'm surprised, Mr. Kastellanos. But I know you make it your business to know everyone."

A faint smile tugged at the corner of his lips, though it didn't reach his eyes. "Only the ones worth knowing."

There was something disconcerting about how easily he slid into her space, as if he belonged there—comfortable, confident, and already calculating.

"I hear Vorlákis Enterprises is eyeing a few acquisitions," he said, swirling the champagne in his glass. "Busy times."

Her lips curled into a polite smile, though her gaze remained guarded. "It's a crowded field, isn't it?"

Soren inclined his head slightly, his expression unreadable. "It is. And Drakov Holdings is attracting...quite a crowd."

Her pulse quickened, though her expression didn't waver. "You seem very interested in Drakov Holdings."

"That's what I do." He gave a small, easy shrug, as if dismantling companies was just another day's work. "Find the cracks, pick up the pieces, rebuild what's worth saving."

"And profit from the rest," she added smoothly.

"Exactly." His smile sharpened. "You understand, then."

"I understand how this works." Kalista's tone was neutral, her expression unreadable. "But that has nothing to do with me."

Soren gave a slight tilt of his head, studying her as if he found her answer...curious. "Doesn't it?"

"No," she said firmly, though the word felt heavier than she wanted. "I design dresses, Mr. Kastellanos. I don't dismantle companies."

"Hmm." He took a slow sip from his glass, eyes never leaving hers. "That's not what I've heard."

Kalista froze for half a second—just enough for him to notice. "What exactly have you heard?"

Soren's smile was small and deliberate, as though he enjoyed testing just how far he could push. "People like to speculate. You know how it is. You're a Vorlákis. Whether you like it or not, that carries weight—people assume things."

She kept her expression steady, though a flicker of unease stirred inside her. "Then they're assuming wrong."

Soren gave a casual shrug. "Maybe. But Marius wasn't known for his business brilliance. A lot of people are wondering how Drakov Holdings held together as long as it did." He let the implication hang between them, watching her carefully.

Kalista's chest tightened. She'd given Marius countless suggestions over the years—ideas she knew had helped him weather more than one crisis. She had assumed no one noticed. Apparently, she was wrong.

"That has nothing to do with me," she repeated, but her voice lacked its earlier sharpness.

Soren's gaze softened, just a little. "You know, a lot of people stay quiet, thinking they don't belong in rooms where decisions get made." He paused for a beat. "Until they realize they've been making those decisions all along."

Kalista opened her mouth to respond, but the words died on her tongue.

He wasn't talking about Marius—or Drakov Holdings. He was talking about her.

"I'm not interested in getting involved," she said finally, though it felt more like a defense than a statement.

Soren gave her the smallest of nods, as if he'd expected exactly that answer. "Fair enough." He stepped back, creating just enough space between them to signal the conversation was over. "But if you change your mind…"

He didn't finish the sentence. He didn't have to.

With a final glance, he slipped back into the crowd, leaving Kalista standing alone.

The ride back to her penthouse was silent, her mind swirling with everything Soren had said—and everything he hadn't.

She'd spent years thinking she wasn't meant to take control of anything beyond her designs. Her job was to stay in her lane, let Marius handle the business, and avoid the family legacy she never asked for.

But Marius hadn't handled anything. And now, somehow, the world knew it.

When she stepped into her penthouse, the city lights twinkling beyond the windows, the folder her father had given her still sat on the counter. Kalista slipped off her heels and approached it, staring down at the names on the list of struggling companies.

Drakov Holdings

She didn't want to be involved. She didn't want to be *her father*. But the idea of Marius walking away from this unscathed—after everything he'd taken from her—made her blood boil.

Her phone buzzed on the counter. She glanced down at the screen:

Unknown Number

> You don't have to play the game. But it's always better to make the first move.

Chapter 2

Kalista stared at the message on her phone for a moment longer, the weight of the words settling over her:

Unknown Number

> You don't have to play the game. But it's always better to make the first move.

She tapped her thumb against the screen, hesitating only for a breath before typing her reply.

Kali

> Let's meet. Tomorrow morning.

The response came almost instantly.

Unknown Number

> 9 AM. Kastellanos Ventures.

Kalista had dressed carefully—black tailored slacks, a silk blouse, and a structured blazer. Professional. Controlled.

When she reached the receptionist, she gave her name. The woman nodded briskly, standing to escort her down a corridor to a glass-walled conference room.

Inside, Soren stood by the window, the morning light casting sharp lines across his suit. He turned as she entered, his gaze locking on hers with the same cool intensity she remembered from the gala.

"Ms. Vorlákis," he greeted her smoothly, gesturing toward the chair at the head of the table. "Punctual. I like that."

Kalista gave a small, polite nod as she sat, setting her bag carefully on the table. She had spent the night organizing her thoughts, going over everything she knew about Drakov Holdings. Now it was time to use it.

"You asked for this meeting," Soren said, taking his seat across from her. His tone was calm but expectant, as if he already knew she wouldn't waste his time. "Let's hear it."

Kalista sat up straight, folding her hands on the table to keep them from fidgeting. "My father is pushing for acquisitions. He sees Drakov Holdings as low-hanging fruit."

Soren's gaze sharpened slightly, though his posture remained relaxed. "And you?"

Kalista held his gaze, her voice steady. "I agree with him. It's a smart move, strategically. Drakov's assets still have value, even if Marius couldn't see it."

Soren leaned back slightly, studying her as if weighing the truth of her words. "So this is about securing an acquisition for Vorlákis Enterprises?"

Kalista gave the faintest shrug, her expression cool. "It's about ensuring the right assets end up in the right hands. And right now, that means preventing Drakov Holdings from collapsing entirely."

His lips twitched—just enough to suggest approval. "Interesting way of putting it. But I'm guessing there's more."

She allowed herself a small smile. "Of course there's more. My father's company is built on design and vision. We know how to create luxury, but

15

expanding our brand means acquiring complementary divisions. Drakov's assets fit, but only if they're reworked correctly."

Soren nodded, clearly following her logic. "And you believe you're the one who can make that happen?"

"Yes," she replied, without hesitation. "The current leadership—Marius—has been reckless, burning through capital with no long-term strategy. He failed to understand that luxury isn't just about image. It's about meaning, about creating something that resonates."

Soren leaned forward slightly, resting his forearms on the table. "Then why come to me, Ms. Vorlákis? If you've already figured out the problem and the solution, why not keep this in-house and run it yourself?"

The question hit with quiet precision, as if testing the depth of her conviction.

Kalista didn't flinch. She had anticipated this—knew that, eventually, she would have to justify her involvement to someone who wasn't interested in personal grudges.

"My father's company isn't in the business of cleaning up someone else's mess," she said smoothly. "Vorlákis Enterprises acquires brands with strong foundations, not ones circling the drain. If we take on Drakov Holdings, it has to be more than salvage work. It has to be a win—and it has to happen fast."

Soren's expression remained impassive, but his gaze sharpened. "So you need someone who specializes in pulling things apart before building them back up."

"Exactly," Kalista replied, her tone steady. "You're known for precision. I need that."

"And in return?" he asked, tilting his head slightly.

Kalista smiled faintly. "You get access to assets that would otherwise fall into someone else's hands. You've already expressed interest in Drakov Holdings. I assume you don't want a bidding war."

Soren gave a soft, thoughtful hum, as though turning her words over in his mind. "It's a smart play," he admitted. "Efficient."

"And it benefits both of us," Kalista added, her voice calm but deliberate.

Soren regarded her in silence for a moment, as if measuring the weight of her words. Then, with a slow nod, he leaned back in his chair. "You've done your homework."

Kalista allowed herself a small, controlled smile. "I told you—I'm ready."

He didn't respond right away, letting the silence stretch between them. "You're confident," he said at last. "I respect that. But this won't be simple."

"I'm not expecting it to be simple," Kalista replied. "But if I'm going to lead, this is how I start."

Soren's lips curled slightly—not quite a smile, but close enough to suggest approval. "Then we begin."

"So," Natalia said, a teasing grin playing on her lips. "How did your first foray into the world of hostile takeovers go?"

The café was a small, cozy spot tucked between office buildings, a welcome refuge from the rain drizzling outside. The warm scent of coffee and baked goods filled the air, soft chatter blending with the occasional clink of ceramic cups.

Kalista leaned back in the booth, fingers curled around her cappuccino. The warmth grounded her after the tense meeting, though her thoughts were still spinning. Across from her, Natalia leaned forward eagerly, her latte nearly finished.

"It was...interesting," Kalista said, swirling the foam in her cup.

Natalia raised an eyebrow, her grin widening. "Come on, you can't just leave it at 'interesting.' Spill."

Kalista let out a soft laugh, glancing out the rain-streaked window. "It was different," she admitted. "I'm used to working in the background. But today..." She paused, choosing her words carefully.

"But today, you were in the spotlight," Natalia finished, giving her a knowing look. "And?"

Kalista allowed herself a small smile. "And...it felt good. Better than I expected."

Natalia gasped dramatically, setting her cup down with a clatter. "Look at you! One meeting, and suddenly you're corporate royalty."

Kalista rolled her eyes, though the grin on her face gave her away. "It's not like that. I'm just testing the waters."

"Uh-huh," Natalia said, her tone playful but warm. "But admit it—you liked it."

Kalista ran her thumb along the edge of the cup, considering. "I liked that he listened. Soren actually took me seriously. It wasn't just about humoring me."

Natalia tilted her head, watching her closely. "Well, yeah. That makes sense —he wouldn't have come to you otherwise, right? The guy doesn't seem like someone who wastes time."

Kalista gave a small nod, swirling the foam in her coffee. "I know, but it still felt...different. I've spent so long keeping my ideas to myself, or only telling Marius. But Soren looked at me like I belonged in the room, like my input actually mattered."

Natalia's lips curled into a wry smile. "Let me guess: Not exactly the vibe you got from Marius?"

Kalista huffed a soft laugh. "Marius barely listened unless it made him look good. I guess I just got used to being in the background."

Natalia leaned forward, resting her chin on her hand. "Well, it's about time someone saw what you're capable of." Her voice was softer now, tinged with warmth. "But be honest—did it freak you out?"

Kalista thought for a moment, the hum of conversation and the soft clink of cups filling the space around them. "Yeah," she admitted, her voice low. "It's weird, stepping into something I thought I didn't want. But at the same time..." She paused, a flicker of excitement flashing in her eyes. "It feels good. Like I'm finally steering things for myself."

Soren sat behind his desk, his eyes fixed on the city skyline. Lysander, lounged in the chair across from him, a smirk tugging at his lips.

"So, you're bringing Marius's ex-fiancée into the game? That's bold, even for you."

Soren didn't look away from the window. "She's more than just his ex. She knows what she's doing."

Lysander leaned back in his chair, a curious smirk spreading across his face. "Yeah, I've heard the whispers. The Vorlákis family's little secret—how Kalista's got the same business instincts as her father but hides behind her sketches." He chuckled softly. "Always wondered if there was truth to it."

Soren's expression remained unchanged, though something flickered in his eyes—an acknowledgment he wouldn't say aloud. "It's not just whispers."

Lysander arched a brow. "So, the princess is a hidden shark after all?"

Soren turned from the window, his gaze cool but deliberate. "She's smart. And more importantly, she's motivated."

Lysander tilted his head, his smirk sharpening. "Motivated to prove herself? Or just motivated to destroy her ex?"

Soren's silence stretched for a moment too long, and Lysander's grin widened. "Ah, there it is. You know as well as I do—personal grudges make things...messy."

Without missing a beat, Soren replied, his voice smooth and controlled. "If this is a grudge, she's good at hiding it."

Lysander leaned forward slightly, resting his elbows on the armrests of the chair. "That's the thing about grudges—they always come out sooner or later. And when they do, they make a hell of a mess."

Soren allowed himself the faintest of smirks, though it didn't reach his eyes. "If emotions were going to be a problem, I would've seen it by now."

Lysander chuckled, shaking his head. "Or maybe she's better at this game than you thought. A Vorlákis through and through."

Soren leaned back in his chair, folding his arms. "She's focused. That's all that matters."

Lysander shot him an amused look. "Focused. Sure. Until she isn't."

Soren's gaze drifted back toward the window, the weight of Lysander's words lingering. He had worked with enough people to know how emotions—especially hidden ones—could derail even the best plans. But Kalista didn't fit the pattern. If this was personal, she wore the mask well. Too well.

"She's not reckless," Soren said quietly, more to himself than to Lysander. "And reckless is what I avoid."

Lysander stood, brushing imaginary lint off his jacket with a grin. "Well, I hope you're right, Ren. Because if she's not reckless...that means she's calculating. And people like that? They're dangerous."

Soren said nothing as Lysander left the room, the door clicking softly behind him.

Chapter 3

Kalista sat across from Soren in the sleek conference room at Kastellanos Ventures, her laptop open between them. The glow from the screen reflected off the glass table, illuminating charts, projections, and forecasts —each carefully designed to tighten the noose around Drakov Holdings.

"Target the niche vendors first," Kalista said, clicking through a list of Drakov's suppliers. "They've been neglected for years. We offer them better terms, something Marius never considered, and they'll abandon him before he knows what hit him."

Soren nodded, his gaze sharp and focused. "And we leak the story to key outlets. Not the major ones—they'll catch on later. We start small, with rumors. That'll spook investors without drawing too much attention at first."

Kalista leaned back, her fingers drumming softly on the table. "Once the smaller clients pull out, Drakov's liquidity issues will become impossible to hide."

Soren's eyes flicked to hers, a hint of approval in his expression. "That's when we move in. Offer just enough hope to force his hand—make him think he can save the company by selling off key assets."

Kalista allowed herself a small smile, though the weight of what they were doing pressed against her chest. This wasn't just dismantling a company. It was precision work, the kind that cut clean and deep.

"And when he sells," she continued, "we pick up exactly what we want. On our terms."

Soren's lips curved slightly. "Efficient."

She gave a short nod, the rush of control settling uneasily within her. There was no going back now. They were making the first move, and if everything went according to plan, Marius would never recover.

Hours later, Kalista watched as Drakov Holdings began to unravel. The digital ticker on her screen blinked relentlessly, each drop in stock value landing like a hammer strike. Vendors had pulled out exactly as they predicted, and the leaked rumors were spreading across smaller business networks, fueling investor panic.

The company was hemorrhaging money, and the stock was in freefall.

Kalista's heart raced as the numbers spiraled downward. Marius had always chased flashy, short-term wins, ignoring the steady, sustainable growth that could have carried him through rough times. Now, the cracks in his empire were on full display.

Soren stood beside her, his arms crossed as he observed the screen. "It's happening faster than I expected," he said, his tone calm but satisfied.

Kalista nodded, though the pit in her stomach tightened. The victory felt...complicated. This was exactly what they had planned, but watching it unfold didn't bring the satisfaction she thought it would.

"You okay?" Soren asked, his gaze flicking to her briefly.

"I'm fine." Kalista forced a smile. "It's just...strange."

"Strange?" Soren's voice was measured, probing without prying.

She exhaled slowly, her fingers tapping lightly on the edge of the table. "I've spent most of my life avoiding this side of things. My family always pushed me toward it, and I ran the other way. Now, here I am, right in the middle of it—taking down a company like I know what I'm doing."

Soren's expression didn't change, but there was a flicker of something—maybe approval—in his eyes. "You do know what you're doing."

Kalista gave a small, humorless laugh. "That's what makes it so weird."

He leaned in slightly, his tone measured. "It's not weird, Kalista. You just didn't expect this to be part of who you are."

The weight of his words settled over her, and for a moment, she let herself sit with that truth. She *hadn't* expected this—had spent years trying to stay in her creative lane, hoping that the business would take care of itself. But now, sitting here with Soren, orchestrating the downfall of Drakov Holdings, she realized something: maybe she wasn't just avoiding responsibility. Maybe she had been afraid to find out what she was capable of.

She straightened in her chair, the hum of the plummeting stock no longer as oppressive. "Maybe," she murmured, more to herself than to Soren. "Maybe it's time I stop pretending this isn't my world."

Soren didn't respond immediately, but the approval in his eyes deepened. "If that's the case, you're already ahead of most people."

Kalista relaxed into the cushioned seat, the tension of the day slipping from her shoulders as the wine was poured. Across from her, Soren's expression was as composed as ever, though a flicker of something softer passed through his eyes.

"It still feels weird," Kalista said, swirling her wine gently in its glass.

Soren tilted his head slightly. "What does?"

"Being taken seriously," she admitted, a wry smile tugging at her lips. "I've spent years being the 'creative one.' People love my designs, but no one ever asked me to sit at the table. Now I'm here...and I keep waiting for someone to tell me I don't belong."

Soren rested his glass on the table, his gaze unwavering. "And yet, here you are. No one's telling you that."

Kalista huffed a soft laugh. "No, they're not. But it's still hard to shake the feeling. It's like I've been waiting for permission that never came."

Soren leaned back slightly, the edges of his mouth curling just enough to suggest amusement. "If you keep waiting for permission, you'll never get it. The ones who succeed are the ones who stop waiting."

His words settled over her, heavier than she expected. She knew he was right—part of her had known it all along. But hearing it from him, from someone who had clawed his way to the top, made it hit differently.

"You're good at this," Soren added after a moment. "Whether you see it or not."

Kalista's lips quirked into a half-smile. "I think that's what surprises me the most." She took a sip of wine, letting the warmth spread through her. "I always told myself I wasn't cut out for this part of the business. But now that I'm here..." She trailed off, her thoughts drifting.

"You realize you can be."

Kalista met his gaze, surprised by the steadiness in his voice. "Yeah. I guess I do."

Soren's eyes remained on hers, unwavering. "That's the hardest part—convincing yourself you belong. The rest is just strategy."

She tilted her glass toward him in mock salute. "Easy for you to say. You've always been good at this."

His smile deepened, though it didn't quite reach his eyes. "Not always."

Kalista raised an eyebrow, intrigued. "No?"

Soren's gaze dropped briefly to his wine glass, a flicker of something thoughtful passing through him. "I had to learn—just like you. There was a time when no one took me seriously, either."

Kalista leaned forward slightly, curiosity piqued. "What changed?"

Soren's lips curved, though the smile was more deliberate now. "I stopped waiting for someone else to see my worth."

The simplicity of his answer caught her off guard, and for a moment, she could see the person beneath the polished exterior—the man who had fought for everything he had.

"Guess that's something I'll have to work on," she said, her voice quieter now.

"You will," Soren said, his tone confident but not unkind.

The conversation drifted after that, easing into lighter topics—snippets of their lives, fleeting observations about the restaurant, and brief moments of shared humor. Kalista found herself laughing at Soren's dry wit, something she hadn't expected to enjoy as much as she did.

By the time they finished the bottle of wine, the restaurant had begun to empty, leaving them in the quiet comfort of their booth. The tension between them was subtle but undeniable—an unspoken current that neither of them seemed ready to acknowledge fully.

Soren stood first, extending his hand. "You did well today, Kalista." His voice was low, and though the words were simple, there was something sincere in the way he said them.

Kalista smiled as she took his hand, the warmth of his grip steadying her. "It's easier with the right partner."

The quiet of her penthouse felt heavier than usual. Kalista slipped off her heels, her bare feet padding softly across the hardwood floor. Exhaustion settled in her limbs now that the adrenaline had worn off.

Her gaze drifted to the sketchbook on the coffee table. She ran her hand over the worn cover, tracing the edges with her fingertips. The pages inside held remnants of the life she thought she wanted—designs she'd once poured her heart into, back when the world felt simpler.

Her phone buzzed, the screen lighting up with Natalia's name. Without hesitation, Kalista answered.

"Hey," she said softly, sinking onto the couch.

"Hey yourself," Natalia replied, her tone light but probing. "So, did you bring the empire to its knees?"

Kalista gave a soft laugh, though it lacked its usual spark. "We made a dent."

Natalia's voice softened, but there was a trace of playful challenge. "Yeah, yeah. But what about you? How do you feel about it?"

Kalista exhaled, her fingers idly flipping the pages of her sketchbook. "Honestly? I don't know."

"Of course you don't," Natalia said gently. "This was never just about business for you, Kali. You've been avoiding this world your whole life, and now, suddenly, you're in the thick of it."

Kalista rubbed her temple, feeling the weight of Natalia's words settle over her. "I thought winning would feel better."

Natalia hummed thoughtfully on the other end. "Winning doesn't always feel good. Especially when it means becoming someone you never thought you'd be."

The truth of that hit Kalista square in the chest. She had stepped into this world not just to dismantle Marius's company but to prove something to herself—and that scared her more than anything.

"I just..." Kalista hesitated, her voice catching. "What if I'm not cut out for this? What if I can't be what everyone expects?"

Natalia's voice was gentle but firm. "You don't have to be what anyone expects. You just have to be you."

"That's the problem." Kalista's laugh was brittle. "I don't even know who that is right now."

Natalia's tone softened, like a steady hand on Kalista's shoulder. "You know more than you think. You've spent years building things, creating things. You know how to make something beautiful from nothing. Now, you just have to figure out how to do that for yourself."

Kalista stared down at the sketchbook, the designs blurring together. "I don't know if I can do both. The creative stuff...and this business side."

"Yes, you can," Natalia said with quiet conviction. "It's not one or the other, Kali. You can be both. You're allowed to be both. And you don't have to figure it all out right now."

Kalista swallowed hard, emotion rising in her throat. "What if I mess it up?"

"Then you mess it up," Natalia said simply. "And you get back up and try again. That's what it means to build something real."

For a moment, Kalista sat in silence, letting Natalia's words sink in. She felt something loosen in her chest—a tightness she hadn't realized she was holding.

"You're always too good at this, you know," Kalista murmured, a faint smile tugging at her lips.

Natalia chuckled softly. "What are best friends for? I've got you, Kali. No matter what."

After they hung up, Kalista sat quietly on the couch, the sketchbook still in her lap. She traced the edge of one of her drawings, the familiar sensation grounding her in a way nothing else could.

Chapter 4

"Kali," Stavros began, folding his hands on the table, his tone carrying the weight of a decision already made. "We need to discuss the future of Vorlákis Enterprises."

Kalista leaned back slightly, steeling herself for the conversation she knew was coming. "I've been working on that," she said, keeping her voice measured. "Kastellanos Ventures and I are coordinating to acquire key assets from Drakov Holdings. We'll both get what we need without competing against each other."

The slight arch of Stavros's brow was his only visible reaction. "So you're working with Soren Kastellanos now?"

"Yes," Kalista said plainly. "It's the most efficient move for everyone."

The polished wood table between them gleamed under the glow of the chandelier. Her father's seat at the head of the table felt heavier than ever— a throne he'd occupied for decades, a legacy she was expected to inherit.

"And yet, you're still avoiding the real work." Stavros's voice remained calm, but the disappointment in it was unmistakable. "This family needs leadership, Kali. Not just deals with Kastellanos."

"I'm securing assets," Kalista replied, her frustration simmering just beneath the surface. "That's leadership, Dad. I'm thinking ahead."

The weight of the house settled around her—a mansion filled with heirlooms and traditions that felt like obligations. The crystal stemware, the silver candlesticks, the antique portrait of her grandparents presiding silently from the far wall—all of it seemed to remind her of the path her father expected her to take.

"That's strategy," Stavros said, waving her off as if it wasn't enough. "But strategy without commitment won't build a future."

Kalista's gaze flicked toward her mother, Evadne, seated gracefully beside Stavros. As always, her mother's expression was composed, unreadable. Evadne had perfected the art of silence—supporting her husband without ever having to say a word.

"I'm still figuring out where I fit," Kalista admitted, shifting slightly in her chair. "This doesn't have to be rushed."

Her father's eyes narrowed. "It does. I've given you time, Kali. But time is running out. The board wants to know what comes next—and so do I."

Kalista's jaw tightened. "That's supposed to be my husband's role."

Stavros leaned forward, his gaze steady and unrelenting. "And where is this husband, Kali? Because the last option didn't work out."

The words hit her harder than she expected. She had built her entire plan around someone else stepping into that role—a plan that had crumbled in her hands.

"That plan failed," Stavros continued, his voice measured but with the weight of finality. "You can't keep waiting for someone else to take on your responsibilities."

Her pulse quickened, frustration bubbling beneath the surface. "I'm not waiting for anyone," she snapped. "I'm working with Soren Kastellanos to secure the assets we need. That's leadership."

Stavros shook his head slowly, disappointment flickering in his eyes. "That's strategy, Kali. Leadership means more than striking deals. What happens when this is over? What happens after Drakov Holdings?"

Kalista clenched her fists beneath the table. "I'm still figuring that out."

"That's not good enough," Stavros said, his voice sharp, though he kept it level. "This company won't wait for you to decide if you want to lead."

Evadne's voice cut through the tension, soft but firm. "Your father is right, darling. You've been preparing for this your whole life—whether you realize it or not."

Kalista glanced between them, anger simmering just beneath the surface. "You're both acting like I don't have a choice."

Stavros gave her a long, measured look. "This is your legacy, Kali. You can't outrun it forever."

The weight of his words settled over her, heavy and inescapable. She hated how easily they dismissed her dreams—how they expected her to surrender her identity for a role she never wanted.

"I just need time," she said, her voice quieter now but no less defiant. "I need time to figure this out on my own terms."

Stavros exhaled slowly, as if conceding the battle but not the war. "Take the time you need. But remember—this company won't wait. And neither will the world."

Kalista leaned her head against the cool metal wall of the elevator, closing her eyes for a brief moment. The hum of the elevator's ascent filled the silence around her, a dull, rhythmic sound that almost drowned out the thoughts spinning in her mind.

The dinner with her parents had left her drained—exhausted in a way no amount of sleep could fix. She needed air, space...something. She needed to be away from the weight of her father's expectations, from the impossible choice between the life she wanted and the legacy she was supposed to uphold.

She hadn't known where else to go. Calling Soren had felt like the only real option, even if it made no sense. He had mentioned once, in passing, that his place was always open if she needed a break. She'd thought it was just something people said, polite but meaningless. Yet somehow, she had ended up here, standing in his elevator, hoping she wasn't making a mistake.

When the doors slid open, Kalista stepped out into the quiet elegance of Soren's penthouse. The polished marble floors gleamed under the soft lighting, and the wide expanse of windows offered a sweeping view of the glittering city below. The space was immaculate, minimalist, with a sense of control woven into every detail—much like the man who lived there.

She heard the faint clink of glass from the kitchen. A moment later, Soren appeared with a tumbler of whiskey in hand, his expression shifting from mild surprise to calm acceptance the instant their eyes met. He didn't ask why she was there. Instead, he simply gave her a nod and gestured toward the couch.

"I figured it would be a long night," he said, setting his drink down on the coffee table and disappearing briefly into the kitchen. When he returned, he had another glass in hand. "Drink?"

Kalista took the offered glass, letting the warmth of the whiskey bleed into her palms. She sat down on the couch, sinking into the soft leather with a sigh. "You make a habit of offering women whiskey at midnight?"

Soren smirked, sitting beside her with his usual quiet composure. "Only the ones I think might actually drink it."

She gave a small, tired laugh, swirling the whiskey in her glass. "Fair enough."

For a moment, neither of them spoke, the silence between them more comfortable than Kalista had expected. The tension from earlier—her father's sharp words, the weight of expectation pressing down on her—felt like it had loosened slightly, slipping away in the quiet hum of the city beyond the windows.

———————◆O◆———————

"My father thinks I'm avoiding responsibility," Kalista said after a moment, her voice quiet but edged with frustration.

Soren leaned back into the cushions, one arm draped casually along the back of the couch. "Is he wrong?"

She shot him a wry glance. "You're supposed to say no."

His lips quirked in amusement. "I don't say what I'm supposed to."

Kalista exhaled slowly, the warmth of the whiskey softening the sharp edges of her thoughts. "It's not that I'm avoiding responsibility," she murmured, more to herself than to him. "It's just...I spent my whole life thinking someone else would do this. It was supposed to be my husband's role."

Soren didn't say anything at first, but the weight of his gaze felt steady, grounding. "And now?"

"And now," she said with a bitter smile, "there's no husband. Just me."

The words hung in the air, heavy and inescapable.

"Your father's a smart man," Soren said slowly, "but that doesn't mean his way is the only way. You don't have to take on this legacy the way he expects you to."

Kalista turned her glass in her hands, staring down at the amber liquid inside. "I just don't want to lose myself in it."

"You won't," Soren said simply. "Not if you lead the way you want to."

His words were calm, steady, but they carried a weight that settled in her chest. It wasn't just the reassurance she needed—it was the possibility that maybe, just maybe, she could carve her own path through this tangled mess of expectations and ambition.

Soren's hand brushed hers—light, fleeting, but deliberate. The warmth of his touch sent a small ripple through her, and for a moment, she let herself rest in it. In the simplicity of that connection, unspoken and uncomplicated.

Her heart pounded in her chest, and she wondered if he could feel it through her skin.

"Soren..." She wasn't even sure what she wanted to say. The words caught somewhere between caution and curiosity, between hesitation and something much harder to ignore.

He didn't move closer, but he didn't pull away either. His blue eyes stayed locked on hers, steady and patient, as if waiting to see which direction she would take.

For a moment, Kalista considered it—letting herself fall into whatever this was, crossing the invisible line between them. It would be easy, and it would feel good. But she wasn't ready.

Not yet.

Soren must have sensed the shift in her, because he gave her hand one last, deliberate squeeze before releasing it. "Not everything needs to happen tonight," he said softly, as if reading her mind.

Kalista nodded, grateful for the out he had given her, even though part of her didn't want to leave.

She stood, smoothing the fabric of her dress as if preparing herself for the world outside this quiet bubble. As she turned toward the door, Soren caught her hand one last time, his grip gentle but firm.

"When the time comes," he murmured, his eyes holding hers, "you'll know what to do."

His words settled over her like a promise—one she wasn't ready to believe just yet, but one she hoped would be true when the time came.

Kalista gave his hand a small, grateful squeeze before stepping away, the cool night air waiting for her on the other side of the door.

Chapter 5

Kalista moved gracefully through the crowd, her arm lightly looped through Soren's, their presence together stirring curious glances from every corner of the room.

Kalista had been to more events like this than she could count—corporate gatherings where deals were disguised as small talk and every conversation was a strategic move. But tonight felt different. The stakes were higher, the atmosphere charged, and the weight of everything she and Soren had been working toward hung in the air like a storm waiting to break.

Every brush of his hand, every glance exchanged, sent a spark through her. She told herself it was just the thrill of the night—the satisfaction of seeing their plans take shape—but a deeper part of her knew better. There was something between them, and tonight, it felt like it might finally come to the surface.

"Enjoying yourself?" Soren's voice was low, warm against her ear as they paused near the edge of the dance floor.

Kalista glanced up at him, pulse quickening beneath the sharp gaze that always seemed to see too much. "Surviving," she said with a small, teasing smile.

He leaned closer, his expression unreadable but intense. "You're doing more than that. They're watching you."

She followed his gaze across the room, noticing the way heads turned toward them—some with curiosity, others with calculation. It didn't matter. For the first time, she felt like she belonged in this world, not as someone's accessory, but as a player in her own right.

A waiter approached with a tray of champagne flutes, and Soren smoothly plucked two, handing one to her. The bubbles fizzed as Kalista took a sip, savoring the crispness that cut through the intensity of the evening.

"So," she asked lightly, raising an eyebrow. "How do you think we're doing?"

Soren gave a faint smile. "They're curious, but no one knows exactly what to make of us yet. That's good."

Kalista nodded, understanding. The whispers were intentional—the rumors of Vorlákis and Kastellanos Ventures working together had stirred intrigue, uncertainty, and fear. It was the kind of uncertainty that gave them an edge, kept everyone guessing just long enough for them to move.

As they drifted further into the room, Soren leaned closer, his voice low. "You've surprised them."

Kalista glanced at him, her heart quickening—not from the champagne or the evening's success, but from the way he looked at her, like she was the most natural person to have by his side.

"They expected to see your father's daughter," Soren continued. "They weren't ready for you."

Kalista felt the warmth of those words settle inside her, quiet but powerful. It wasn't just approval—it was recognition. She had spent years fighting to feel seen, to be more than the daughter groomed to take over an empire she wasn't sure she wanted. Tonight, standing beside Soren, she knew she had crossed some invisible line.

Still, the evening pressed on, the weight of everything riding on tonight lurking beneath the surface of each conversation. The thought of it lingered at the edges of her mind, enough to make her chest tighten with the need to catch her breath—not from fear, but from the realization of how far she'd come.

Kalista set her empty glass on a nearby table and gave Soren a small, almost conspiratorial smile. "Come with me," she whispered, tugging lightly at his sleeve.

Soren's gaze flicked over her, curiosity and amusement dancing in his expression. Without a word, he followed her through the sea of guests.

The night air felt cool and crisp as they stepped out onto the balcony, the noise of the ballroom muffled behind them. Kalista rested her hands on the smooth stone railing, taking a deep breath as the lights of the city stretched out below.

It wasn't about needing to escape, she realized. It was about claiming a moment for herself.

Soren stood beside her, hands resting loosely on the railing, his presence steady as always. "You're doing well," he said, his voice low. "Better than well, actually."

Kalista smiled, glancing at him. "It still feels surreal," she admitted. "Being part of this world, not just watching from the sidelines."

Soren turned his head slightly, studying her. "You've been more than a spectator for a long time, Kalista. You just hadn't realized it yet."

The words settled over her with a quiet finality, and she knew he was right. She had been part of this world—offering ideas, making decisions—long before anyone had noticed, even herself. Now, there was no hiding from it.

"You don't have to wait for permission," Soren added, his voice soft but deliberate. "Not from your father. Not from anyone."

Her breath hitched slightly at the truth of it. She had been waiting—for years—for someone else to tell her it was okay to want more. To be more. But she didn't need anyone's permission, not anymore.

For a moment, the two of them stood in comfortable silence, the hum of the city filling the quiet between them. It wasn't the same silence she felt with her parents—a silence heavy with unspoken expectations. This was different. It was the kind of silence where she could breathe, where she could be.

Soren shifted closer, just enough that their shoulders brushed. His hand lifted, his thumb brushing gently along her jaw, the touch sending a ripple of warmth through her. "Kalista…"

Her name had never sounded like that before—like a promise and a question all at once. She felt it settle deep within her, stirring something that had long been dormant.

"No one calls me that," she whispered, though she didn't pull away from his touch.

Soren's thumb lingered just a moment longer before retreating, his gaze steady and calm. "Do you mind if I do?"

Kalista smiled softly, a quiet warmth blooming in her chest. "You can call me Kali."

The corners of Soren's mouth twitched in a ghost of a smile. "Then you can call me Ren."

"Ren…" She tested the name, letting it roll off her tongue in a way that felt oddly natural.

Something flickered in his expression—something that looked a little like satisfaction, as if this exchange, small as it was, had closed the distance between them in a way that words alone never could.

For a moment, she considered closing the distance between them, leaning into the quiet pull she felt whenever she was around him. It would have been easy to let herself get lost in whatever this was between them.

But the thought was interrupted by the distant hum of voices behind them —a reminder of the world they were still a part of. Kalista smiled, stepping back slightly, the spell between them gently broken.

Soren's gaze lingered on her, sharp and searching, as if he was waiting to see what she would do next. But he didn't press.

"We should go back in," she said softly, though a part of her wanted to stay out here with him, in this quiet moment where the world felt just a little simpler.

Soren gave a small nod, his expression unreadable but not unkind. "After you."

———◆O◆———

Kalista slipped through the crowd, the warmth and noise of the ballroom washing over her. She hadn't gone far when she felt someone step into her path.

Marius.

Her pulse quickened, but not with fear. This was anger—raw and simmering just beneath the surface. He looked just as smug as ever, though his eyes held a sharp edge now, glinting with bitterness.

"Kali." His voice was low, the forced charm barely masking the anger simmering underneath. "We need to talk."

Kalista folded her arms, her stance unwavering. "There's nothing to talk about, Marius."

His jaw tightened, his polished veneer beginning to crack. "Don't play dumb. I know what you're doing." He stepped closer, his voice a venomous whisper. "You and Kastellanos—working together to destroy me."

Kalista held her ground, raising an eyebrow. "You destroyed yourself. I just gave things a little push."

Marius's hand shot out, gripping her arm—not with the gentleness she once thought she knew, but with a force that made her skin crawl. "You think you can walk away from everything we built?" His voice was sharp, desperate. "You think Kastellanos cares about you? You're just a pawn in his game, Kali. He'll use you and toss you aside the second you're not useful."

The words stung, but only for a moment. Then, something deeper—something fierce—rose within her.

Kalista yanked her arm free, her voice steady, cutting. "I'm not a pawn, Marius. In fact, I'm the one who came up with the plan to bring down

Drakov Holdings."

Marius blinked, stunned into silence for the first time.

Kalista pressed forward, her voice low but filled with satisfaction. "Ren only wanted a few scraps of information at first. I was the one who saw the opportunity. I was the one who suggested we work together." She gave a small, sharp smile. "So no, Marius. I'm not just along for the ride—I'm steering it."

The color drained from his face, the realization sinking in. "You...?" His voice cracked slightly, disbelief replacing his arrogance. "You did this?"

Kalista's smile deepened, razor-sharp. "I warned you not to underestimate me. But you never listened, did you?"

Before Marius could respond, a shadow fell over them—calm, composed, and dangerous.

Soren.

He moved smoothly between them, his presence cold and unyielding, like a wall that Marius would never climb. "Is there a problem here?" Soren's voice was low, deliberate, carrying the weight of a man used to being obeyed.

Marius sneered, but the fury in his eyes wavered under Soren's gaze. He took a step back, jaw clenched. "This isn't over," he muttered, his bravado fraying at the edges.

Soren's expression didn't change. His voice remained calm, almost bored. "It is. Walk away."

Marius's fists clenched at his sides, but the fight had already left him. With one last glare—directed equally at Kalista and Soren—he turned on his heel and stalked away, his retreat as bitter as the words he left unsaid.

The tension lingered in the air, heavy and charged. For a moment, neither Kalista nor Soren moved, the sound of Marius's footsteps fading into the distant hum of the ballroom.

Kalista exhaled slowly, the adrenaline still thrumming beneath her skin. She felt Soren's gaze on her, steady and unflinching, as if waiting to see if she would break. But she didn't.

"Are you okay?" Soren's voice was low, his hand brushing lightly against her arm—not as a question of doubt, but as a quiet offering of comfort.

Kalista nodded, though her heart was still racing. "I'm fine. I can handle him."

Soren gave a small, almost imperceptible nod. "I know you can."

His words weren't just reassurance—they were acknowledgment. Recognition. He had seen her face down Marius without flinching, had heard the way she claimed the plan as her own. And now, standing beside her, he wasn't stepping in to protect her—he was standing with her. As her equal.

Kalista's gaze softened, the tension that had coiled in her chest loosening slightly. She had expected Marius to come after her eventually—had braced herself for the confrontation. But what she hadn't expected was the strange sense of relief that followed.

This wasn't just about bringing down Drakov Holdings anymore. It was about proving to herself that she belonged in this world—not as someone's fiancée or accessory, but as a force in her own right.

"Thank you," she said quietly, her voice steady but warm.

Soren gave her a small, knowing smile, the kind that said he understood without needing to say it aloud. "Always."

For a moment, the world seemed to pause, the weight of the evening lifting just enough for her to breathe.

Kalista squared her shoulders, letting the confidence settle deeper into her bones. She wasn't running anymore. This was her world now, and she was ready to claim it.

"Come on," Soren said, his hand brushing hers in a fleeting, deliberate gesture. "We've got a gala to finish."

Soren let his hand linger on Kalista's as he led her toward the waiting car, but when she stopped just shy of stepping outside, he knew she wasn't quite ready to leave.

He wasn't either.

The car waited at the curb, but the space between them still hummed with all the things left unsaid. The cool breeze tousled a loose strand of Kalista's dark hair, and without thinking, Soren reached out, tucking it gently behind her ear.

"Kali..." His voice was low, deliberate, as though saying her name could anchor the moment.

Her lips parted slightly, her breath catching in her throat. "Ren," she whispered, testing the name she'd only just given him permission to use.

That single word—just his name—undid something in him.

Soren's thumb brushed her cheek, lingering for a moment too long, as if caught in a current he couldn't fight. He should've stepped away then. He knew it. He told himself he would.

But when she leaned the slightest bit closer, her gaze flickering between his eyes and his lips, the pull between them became impossible to resist.

He didn't think. He acted.

Their lips met in a slow, deliberate kiss—tentative at first, as if testing the edges of something fragile. But the moment Kalista responded, pressing into him, the kiss deepened, hungry and insistent, breaking through every unspoken boundary they'd carefully tried to keep intact.

Her hands gripped the front of his jacket, and Soren pulled her closer, one hand cupping the back of her neck, the other resting lightly against her hip. The feel of her—soft, warm, alive—made the world narrow to just this moment.

It wasn't reckless. It was inevitable.

But as the kiss lingered, the weight of it began to sink in—what it meant, what it could complicate. And just as the thought formed, Soren forced himself to pull away.

His forehead rested briefly against hers, their breaths mingling in the cool night air.

"This...isn't simple," he whispered, his voice rough from the effort of restraint.

Kalista's fingers loosened their grip on his jacket, her gaze still hazy with the remnants of the kiss. "No," she murmured. "It's not."

For a moment, they stood there—caught between what had just happened and what it meant. And though neither of them moved to close the distance again, the space between them felt charged, alive with the promise of something more.

Soren took a slow step back, his voice soft but firm. "Goodnight, Kali."

Her lips curved into a small, knowing smile—one that sent a shiver down his spine. "Goodnight, Ren."

And with that, she turned, slipping gracefully into the waiting car. Soren stood at the curb, watching the vehicle disappear into the night, the lingering taste of her kiss etched into his mind like a brand.

Chapter 6

The cold marble countertop grounded Soren as he leaned into it, elbows resting heavily against the surface. Beyond the windows, the city sprawled in an endless sea of lights, shimmering against the dark sky like distant constellations. But the view offered no comfort, only the disorienting sense that he was standing at the edge of something dangerous.

He swirled the whiskey in his glass, watching the amber liquid catch the light. Control had always been his anchor. It was the foundation of his success—his ability to compartmentalize, to stay two steps ahead, unaffected by sentiment. Emotions, attachments, they only complicated things.

But Kalista Vorlákis was not supposed to become complicated.

The kiss haunted him—the feel of her, the fire in her touch. It wasn't just the kiss itself but the emotions it had stirred—ones he thought he had buried long ago. For years, he had kept himself closed off, focused solely on the next move, the next acquisition. Vulnerability was a weakness he couldn't afford.

And yet, Kalista wasn't weakness. She was strength, in ways that surprised even him. She wasn't a distraction—she was something more. Something dangerous.

He exhaled sharply, pressing his glass against his forehead. He had been burned before—had trusted someone only to be discarded once he had served his purpose. It had been a hard lesson, one he swore he wouldn't repeat.

But with Kalista...

He wasn't sure he had a choice.

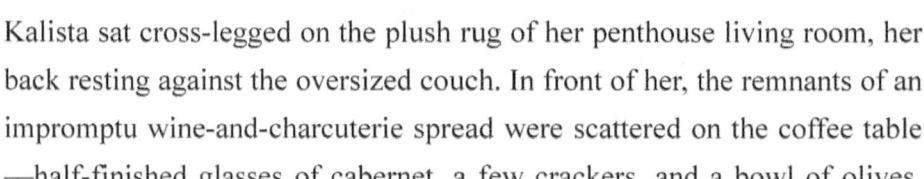

Kalista sat cross-legged on the plush rug of her penthouse living room, her back resting against the oversized couch. In front of her, the remnants of an impromptu wine-and-charcuterie spread were scattered on the coffee table —half-finished glasses of cabernet, a few crackers, and a bowl of olives. Across from her, Natalia reclined comfortably on the couch, her feet tucked under her, wearing the smug expression of someone who knew exactly what was coming next.

"So," Natalia said, swirling the wine in her glass with a mischievous glint in her eye. "Are you going to tell me what's going on, or should I start guessing?"

Kalista sighed, setting her own glass down with a soft clink. She had invited Natalia over for advice—or maybe just reassurance—but now, sitting here with her best friend's expectant gaze locked onto her, the words felt harder to say than she had anticipated.

"It's...complicated," Kalista began, tugging her knees closer to her chest.

Natalia arched a brow. "Complicated? You kissed Soren, didn't you?"

Kalista's head snapped up, her cheeks warming. "How—"

"Please." Natalia waved a dismissive hand, grinning. "It's obvious. The way you've been talking about him lately? The tension? The *eyes*? You didn't stand a chance."

Kalista groaned, burying her face in her hands. "We kissed. Okay? It just...happened."

Natalia leaned forward, resting her chin on her hand, her expression softening with genuine curiosity. "And how do you feel about it?"

Kalista let her hands drop, her gaze drifting to the city skyline visible through the floor-to-ceiling windows. The kiss had stirred something deep inside her—a spark she hadn't felt in a long time. But with it came uncertainty, fear. "I like him," she admitted, the words barely more than a whisper. "More than I thought I would. But after everything with Marius...I don't know if I can trust myself to feel this way again."

Natalia's playful expression softened into one of quiet understanding. "That's fair. Marius did a number on you. It's only natural to be scared."

Kalista picked at the hem of her sweater, her voice small. "What if it's just...a rebound? What if I'm just replacing one mistake with another?"

Natalia set her glass down and leaned forward, resting her hand over Kalista's. "Kali, this isn't Marius. Soren isn't some selfish narcissist who's only in it for himself. He sees you. He respects you. That's different."

Kalista's throat tightened. "But what if it's too soon? What if I ruin this, too?"

Natalia's grip on her hand tightened, her voice steady and sure. "Then you take it slow. You don't have to figure everything out right now. Just...give yourself permission to feel, Kali. Even if it's scary."

Kalista swallowed hard, the knot in her chest loosening just a fraction. Trusting someone again felt like standing at the edge of a cliff, unsure whether she was about to fly or fall. But sitting here with Tali, a flicker of hope began to take root.

"You really think it's okay?" Kalista asked, her voice barely above a whisper.

Natalia gave her a soft, encouraging smile. "It's more than okay. Just promise me one thing—don't let fear make decisions for you. You've got this, Kali. One step at a time."

Kalista nodded, the weight on her chest lifting slightly. Maybe Natalia was right. Maybe it was okay to lean into the unknown, even if it scared her.

And maybe—just maybe—Soren was worth the risk.

The boardroom at Vorlákis Enterprises glowed with morning light, casting sharp lines across the glass walls. Kalista sat at the long conference table, laptop open, but her thoughts drifted dangerously far from the meeting at hand.

Across from her, Soren sat with his usual calm precision, flipping through the proposal documents. But there was a tension in him today, subtle but unmistakable. The sharp line of his jaw, the way his gaze lingered on her just a second too long—it all pointed to the same thing: the kiss.

"The next step," Soren said, breaking the silence, "is to secure Drakov's luxury division before it goes to auction." His voice was smooth, controlled, but there was an edge beneath it—an edge Kalista hadn't heard before.

She nodded, forcing herself to focus. "Agreed. But we need to tread carefully. Marius is desperate, and desperate men make reckless moves."

Ren's jaw ticked, his gaze hardening. "I can handle Marius."

There it was—that sharpness again, cutting through the conversation like a knife. Kalista bristled, her irritation rising.

"I know you can," she replied evenly. "But we can't just barrel through this. We need to be strategic."

Soren leaned back slightly, folding his arms. "I *am* being strategic."

The air between them crackled with unspoken tension. This wasn't just about Drakov Holdings. The kiss lingered in the room with them, a shadow neither could shake.

Kalista took a breath, softening her tone. "Ren, I'm not questioning your abilities. I just...I don't want things to get messy."

Soren's eyes darkened, and for a moment, Kalista saw something flicker behind his gaze—something raw and unresolved. "Things are already messy," he said quietly.

The weight of his words settled heavily between them. This wasn't just about business anymore. This was about them—about whatever it was they were becoming.

Kalista opened her mouth to respond, but before she could find the words, Soren closed the file in front of him with a decisive snap. "We'll pick this up tomorrow. I have another meeting."

He stood, gathering his things with practiced precision, his expression unreadable once again. For a moment, Kalista thought he might say something more—something about the kiss, about the tension between them—but he didn't.

And then he was gone, leaving her alone in the boardroom, her heart pounding and her thoughts spiraling.

Kalista sat motionless, the weight of the conversation—and everything unsaid—settling around her like a thick fog. She stared at the empty chair where Soren had been, her mind replaying his words: *Things are already messy.*

She had known, from the moment they kissed, that this was no longer just business. But knowing it and accepting it were two very different things.

With a sigh, she closed her laptop and leaned back in her chair, her gaze drifting toward the city skyline beyond the glass walls. She wasn't sure how to move forward—not with the acquisition, not with Soren.

Kalista sat on the edge of her bed, the dim city lights flickering through the curtains. Her thumb hovered over her phone screen, heart racing as doubt curled in her chest. She wasn't used to feeling this unsure—not when it came to anyone else. But Soren wasn't like anyone else.

Do I really want to do this?

She exhaled slowly, the thought lingering. Before she could second-guess herself any further, she tapped out the message:

Kali

Are we okay?

The screen stayed still for a moment, the absence of a response pressing against her ribs like a weight. She stared at the words, a knot tightening in her stomach. The message had been a gamble—a way to clear the air or make things worse.

Then, her phone buzzed. **Ren is calling.**

Her pulse kicked up as she answered, pressing the phone to her ear. "Hey."

"Hey," Soren murmured. His voice was low, carrying the hint of fatigue but with an undeniable steadiness.

For a moment, neither of them said anything, the silence between them thick with everything unspoken.

"I wasn't expecting you to call," Kalista admitted, tucking her hair behind her ear.

"I figured it would be easier than dancing around this over text," Soren replied, his voice lighter, though still edged with that seriousness she'd come to recognize.

Kalista couldn't help but smile, even though her heart was pounding. "You do have a point."

Another pause settled between them—not the awkward kind, but one filled with the weight of things neither of them had quite figured out how to say.

Soren broke the silence first. "You asked if we're okay."

"Yeah," she whispered. "Are we?"

There was a long, deliberate pause. "We are if you want us to be."

Kalista closed her eyes, the knot in her chest loosening just a bit. "I don't regret the kiss, Ren," she said quietly, the words slipping from her before she could stop them.

On the other end of the line, she heard him exhale slowly, the sound almost like relief. "Neither do I."

Her heart skipped, the warmth in his voice settling deep inside her. "But I'm scared," she confessed. "I don't want to make the same mistakes."

"I get that." Soren's voice softened. "Trust me, Kali. I've been there."

The honesty in his words made her throat tighten. "So...what do we do now?"

"We figure it out," Soren said simply. "No pressure, no rush. Just one step at a time."

Kalista smiled at the quiet reassurance in his tone. "You make it sound easy."

"Maybe it doesn't have to be as hard as we think," Soren offered. "We just need to be honest with each other."

She nodded, even though he couldn't see it. "Deal."

For a moment, they lingered in the silence, the sound of his steady breathing on the other end somehow comforting.

"You should get some sleep, Kali," Soren murmured, his voice low, warm, and a little rough around the edges.

Kalista smiled softly, biting her lip. "You too, Ren. No all-nighters."

He chuckled, a quiet, genuine sound that made her heart flutter. "No promises. But I'll try."

A comfortable pause followed, the kind of silence that made it hard to end the call.

"Goodnight, Kali," Soren said, his voice softer now, almost hesitant.

Kalista hesitated for just a moment, then let herself lean into the truth of it. "Goodnight, Ren...and thanks."

"For what?"

She smiled, though he couldn't see it. "For calling instead of texting."

His answer was a low hum, warm and amused. "I told you—I don't like dancing around things."

"Guess I'll have to get used to that," she teased.

"You will," Soren replied, his tone easy but laced with something deeper.

Another beat passed between them, like neither wanted to be the first to hang up.

"Talk soon?" Kalista whispered.

"Count on it," Soren replied, his voice steady, as if he was making a promise that carried more weight than the words suggested.

And with that, the call ended—quietly, without fanfare.

Chapter 7

"What's your endgame, Kalista?"

The question hung in the air, cutting through the quiet tension of the Vorlákis Enterprises boardroom.

Kalista lifted her gaze, meeting the sharp, skeptical eyes of Mr. Karras. Around the table, the other board members shifted in their seats, watching her closely, waiting to see if she would falter. But Kalista didn't flinch.

"My endgame," she replied, her voice calm but deliberate, "is to secure the future of this company by taking what Marius wasted and making it profitable again. And I intend to do that by acquiring Drakov's luxury division before it slips through our fingers."

Soren, seated to her right, gave the slightest nod of approval. It was a small gesture, but enough to settle the hum of adrenaline running beneath her skin. She wasn't just presenting a plan today—she was staking her claim, proving to everyone in the room that she belonged at this table.

Karras leaned forward, folding his hands on the table. "And if Kastellanos Ventures gets there first?"

"They won't." Kalista's answer came without hesitation. "I've coordinated with Mr. Kastellanos to ensure that won't happen."

At the sound of his name, the room shifted. A few board members exchanged uneasy glances, and the weight of skepticism settled over the table like a heavy cloud. Soren's reputation preceded him—ruthless, strategic, always three steps ahead. If Kastellanos Ventures was involved, everyone knew the stakes were high.

"Ms. Vorlákis is right," Soren spoke then, his voice smooth and controlled. "If Vorlákis Enterprises doesn't move now, Kastellanos Ventures will. And if I take those assets, they'll be out of your reach permanently."

A murmur rippled through the boardroom, the reality of the situation sinking in.

Karras narrowed his eyes but leaned back in his chair, conceding—for now. "Alright. Let's hear the rest of your plan."

Kalista exhaled slowly, allowing herself a quiet, steadying breath. She glanced at Mr. Kastellanos, whose calm expression didn't falter, and then returned her focus to the board.

"We'll move quickly," she began, her voice clear and confident. "Drakov's luxury division has been underperforming because it failed to tap into niche markets. We already have the infrastructure to leverage those markets—this acquisition will expand our brand without the need to build from scratch."

Mrs. Papadakis, a veteran on the board with a sharp eye for opportunity, nodded thoughtfully. "The Drakov name still holds value. With the right leadership, it could be revitalized."

"And that leadership," Kalista said firmly, "is us."

Karras crossed his arms. "And what if the division is more damaged than it looks? What if Marius's mistakes run deeper than you think?"

Kalista's pulse quickened, but she didn't let it show. This was the moment to stand firm, to show them she was more than just a figurehead in the family business. "I know Drakov Holdings inside and out. I've spent years watching it fail from the inside. I know their strengths—and their vulnerabilities. If we don't act, someone else will."

She glanced toward Mr. Kastellanos for just a beat, and he caught the look, holding her gaze for half a second longer than necessary.

"Someone like me," Soren added smoothly, leaning back in his chair with an air of quiet authority.

The weight of his words settled over the room like a silent warning. There was no time for second-guessing.

For a moment, silence filled the space, tension thick in the air. Then, with a small grunt, Mr. Karras gave a begrudging nod. "Alright, Ms. Vorlákis. We'll back the plan."

Relief flooded Kalista's chest, though she kept her expression composed. The board members began to murmur their approval, their voices blending into a low hum of conversation. Slowly, they gathered their things, filing out of the room one by one.

When the last of them disappeared through the door, leaving her alone with Mr. Kastellanos, Kalista allowed herself a quiet exhale, her hands unclenching from the chair's armrests.

"You handled that well," Soren said, his voice low and steady.

Kalista glanced at him, a flicker of gratitude in her eyes. "I wasn't sure they'd go for it."

"They went for it because they trust you," he replied. "You earned that."

She met his gaze, the unspoken weight of everything between them settling into the space. "And what about you?" she asked softly. "Do you trust me?"

Soren's eyes darkened, a flicker of something unreadable passing over his face. His response was quiet but deliberate. "More than I should."

The soft clink of silverware filled the space between them, candlelight flickering across the sleek surfaces of Soren's penthouse. The meal had cooled, the wine nearly gone, but neither of them seemed to care. The weight of the day's events lingered between them, unspoken but heavy with meaning.

Soren leaned back in his chair, swirling the wine in his glass. "You handled the meeting today like you've been doing it your whole life."

Kalista let out a small breath, her fingers tracing the edge of her wineglass. "I was nervous," she admitted. "I've never led something like that before. I kept thinking I was going to say the wrong thing."

Soren gave a faint smile, the kind that didn't quite reach his eyes but carried a warmth she was beginning to understand. "You didn't. They listened because they knew you knew what you were talking about."

Kalista toyed with the stem of her glass, trying to shake the tension that still clung to her. "I guess I just didn't expect it to feel so...big. Like every word mattered."

Soren set his glass down, his gaze steady. "That's because it did. And you nailed it."

His quiet confidence settled over her, soothing the doubts still stirring in the back of her mind. But even in the calm, there was an unspoken tension between them—one that had lingered since the kiss, since the moment he pulled back the next day.

Kalista tilted her head slightly, her voice soft but curious. "You seemed distant when we were working on the strategy for the meeting. I didn't bring it up on the phone, but we promised honesty..." She trailed off for a moment, studying him. "Was it something I did? Something I can do to help?"

Soren's expression shifted, his jaw tightening briefly before he exhaled, as if bracing himself. "No," he said quietly. "It wasn't you. You didn't do anything wrong."

Kalista stayed silent, letting him find the words.

"There was someone," he began, his voice low but edged with old wounds. "A long time ago. We were engaged. Her name was Isabelle."

Kalista's chest tightened, a pang of something sharp and unexpected flaring within her.

"We built a business together—or at least, that's what I thought." His gaze dropped briefly to the candlelight, shadows playing across his features. "But Isabelle didn't love me. She loved what I could offer her. Once she got what she wanted—clients, deals—she left."

He leaned back in his chair, fingers tapping absently against the glass. "It hit me hard. I learned not to let anyone get that close again. Emotions make you vulnerable, and being vulnerable..." He shook his head, his voice turning sharper. "It cost me everything."

Kalista reached across the table, resting her hand lightly over his. "Ren..."

"I didn't mean to shut you out," he said, his thumb brushing over her knuckles. "I guess old habits die hard."

She squeezed his hand gently. "I understand. But I'm not Isabelle, and I'm not going to leave just because things get difficult."

Soren met her gaze, the tension in his shoulders easing slightly. "I know. That's what scares me."

The honesty in his voice tugged at her heart, and for a moment, they sat in comfortable silence, his hand warm beneath hers.

"You don't have to do this alone," she whispered, the words soft but steady. "I know it's hard to trust again, but I'm here. We'll figure it out—together."

Soren's gaze softened, a flicker of vulnerability in his eyes. "I want that," he admitted. "More than I thought I could."

A quiet smile spread across Kalista's lips. "Then we'll take it one step at a time."

For a moment, the world outside faded, leaving only the two of them. Soren leaned in, and when his lips brushed against hers, it wasn't a promise of more but a quiet reassurance. The kiss was tender, unhurried—a way of saying he would try, even if it scared him.

When they pulled back, their foreheads rested together, the silence between them no longer heavy but peaceful.

"I'm trying," Soren whispered, his breath warm against her skin.

Kalista smiled softly, her hand still tangled in his. "That's all I need."

Ren kissed her hand, a gentle, fleeting gesture that sent a quiet warmth through her.

Chapter 8

"Hello, Ren."

Soren's blood ran cold at the sound of the voice—smooth, sharp, and unsettlingly familiar. He didn't need to turn to know who it was.

Isabelle Novak

When he did face her, she was just as he remembered—elegant, poised, and every bit as dangerous. Draped in black silk, her raven hair swept away from her sharp cheekbones, she smiled with the kind of ease that masked something much darker.

"What are you doing here, Isabelle?" Soren's voice was calm, but his muscles coiled tight.

Her crimson lips curled. "Pravus Group was invited. I thought I'd make an appearance."

His jaw clenched. Of course, *Pravus Group*—her latest hunting ground. Isabelle didn't show up without a reason.

"You always did like to crash parties," Soren muttered.

She laughed softly, the sound like a blade sliding from a sheath. "And you always did hate surprises."

Soren crossed his arms, keeping his voice cool. "What do you want, Isabelle?"

She stepped closer, her perfume—jasmine with an edge of smoke—filling the space between them. "We both know this night isn't just for cocktails and pleasantries," she murmured. "Pravus is moving on Drakov Holdings. But I imagine you've already guessed that."

Soren's eyes narrowed. "If you're here to make threats, don't waste your breath."

Isabelle's smile widened, slow and predatory. "Oh, Ren. I'm not here to threaten you. I'm here to warn you."

Soren arched a brow, unmoved. "Is that what we're calling it now?"

Her gaze glittered with something dangerous. "Let's not pretend we're enemies. I know how you operate—you keep things clean, professional. You avoid drama." She leaned in just enough to lower her voice to a conspiratorial whisper. "But how long do you think you can keep that up?"

Soren's expression didn't change, but tension rippled through him. "I don't play games, Isabelle."

"Oh, but the media loves games," Isabelle purred, tilting her head. "Imagine this headline: *'Heiress Kalista Vorlákis and Soren Kastellanos—From Merger to Scandal?'* They'd eat it up."

Soren's blood ran cold, but he kept his face neutral. Isabelle's smile deepened, sensing the flicker of unease beneath his mask.

"Don't worry," she whispered, brushing a hand lightly over his lapel. "It doesn't have to get that far. Just step aside. Let Pravus take Drakov Holdings, and I'll make sure no one ever hears a whisper of trouble about you and Kalista."

Soren's fists clenched at his sides. "Stay out of this, Isabelle."

Her eyes gleamed, a cruel kind of satisfaction dancing within them. "I wish I could. But you've always had such terrible timing, Ren." She gave him a slow, knowing smile. "And Kalista...well, the press loves a good fall from grace. I wonder how she'll handle it when they start digging into her past—and yours."

The air between them thickened with the weight of her words. Isabelle knew exactly where to strike—subtle, precise, just enough to plant seeds of doubt and chaos.

Soren took a step closer, his voice dropping to a warning growl. "You come near her, and you'll regret it."

Isabelle's smile didn't waver, but her eyes flashed with triumph. "We both know how this ends, Ren. You can't outrun it forever."

With a lingering glance and a playful brush of her fingertips against his sleeve, Isabelle turned and walked away, her dress trailing behind her like the shadow of a storm.

Soren stood rooted in place, fury simmering beneath his skin. Isabelle's threat wasn't direct, but it was no less dangerous. She was setting a trap— and if he wasn't careful, Kalista would end up caught in it.

Stavros set down his wine glass with deliberate care, his sharp gaze settling on his daughter. "I've heard things, Kali."

Kalista met his eyes evenly, though her pulse quickened. "What kind of things?"

Stavros folded his hands together, his expression cool but deliberate. "Rumors. About you and Soren Kastellanos. People are already talking. And when you and a man like him are involved, idle speculation has a way of turning into reality."

Evadne, seated beside him, offered a gentle, sympathetic look. "We only want you to be careful, darling. You know how these things can spiral."

Kalista straightened, keeping her voice calm. "Ren and I are taking things slow. We're being cautious."

Stavros arched an eyebrow, unimpressed. "That's what you thought with Marius, wasn't it? And look how that ended."

The familiar sting of the past struck deep, and Kalista gripped the edge of the table, holding herself steady. "That was different," she said, forcing the words out evenly.

"Was it?" Stavros's tone remained cold, but there was a warning beneath it. "You believed you knew Marius—trusted him—and it didn't stop him from betraying you."

Kalista tightened her grip on the edge of the table. "I left Marius because he cheated," Kalista said softly, though her voice carried an edge of steel. "I wasn't going to stay in a relationship built on lies."

"And now," Stavros continued, undeterred, "you're telling me you're ready to step into something just as risky—this time with Kastellanos? Another man whose interests might not always align with yours?"

Kalista held his gaze, anger simmering just beneath the surface. "Ren isn't Marius."

Stavros leaned back, his eyes narrowing. "No, but he's still a businessman. And businessmen, Kali, always act in their own best interest."

Evadne tilted her head, her expression soft but concerned. "Even if Soren cares about you, his priorities can shift, darling. When business and personal relationships mix, the lines blur. It becomes harder to make the right decisions."

Kalista drew in a slow breath, determined to keep her frustration in check. "I know the risks. I know how to protect myself."

Stavros's gaze remained cold and steady. "You thought you knew with Marius, too."

The words stung more than she cared to admit. But she wasn't the same person she'd been back then—unsure, easily swayed by promises that didn't mean anything. She had learned the hard way that trust was fragile.

"This isn't the same," Kalista said firmly. "Ren and I understand what we're getting into. We're being careful."

Evadne gave her daughter a small, knowing smile. "We don't doubt that you believe you're in control, darling. But emotions have a way of sneaking up on us. When the lines blur, business decisions can become...complicated."

Kalista leaned forward, her voice measured but unwavering. "I appreciate the concern. But this is my decision. I won't live in fear of what *might* happen."

Stavros's expression darkened, disappointment flickering in his eyes. "Just remember—if things go wrong, it won't just be you who pays the price. This family can't afford another mistake."

The weight of his words settled heavily over the table, pressing down like the legacy she had carried her whole life.

"I understand," Kalista said quietly, her voice steady but edged with resolve. "But I'm not going to push Ren away just because of what happened with Marius."

For a moment, Stavros studied her, the silence thick and oppressive. Then, with a slow nod, he leaned back in his chair, conceding—for now.

"We only want what's best for you," Evadne added gently, though her eyes carried the same unspoken warning as her husband's.

Kalista gave a small, polite smile—one that felt more like a shield than anything else. "I know."

The conversation shifted after that, back to the safety of business projections and upcoming ventures. But Kalista's mind remained elsewhere, her father's words echoing in her head.

Marius had been a mistake—one she had learned from. But Soren wasn't Marius. And she wasn't the same person who had been fooled by promises and charm.

"You're being quiet," Kalista said, her voice gentle but curious as she watched Soren stand stiffly by the windows.

He didn't respond right away, his gaze fixed on the glowing skyline. His hands were shoved deep into his pockets, and his jaw was set—his usual composure wrapped tight around him like armor.

Kalista tilted her head slightly, waiting. "Ren?"

"I'm fine," he muttered, though the words sounded hollow.

She crossed her arms, leaning against the kitchen island. "That's not really an answer."

Soren exhaled sharply through his nose, still not looking at her. "It's been a long day."

Kalista took a slow step closer, watching the tension coil through his shoulders. "You didn't seem fine at the gala," she said softly, keeping her voice steady but leaving room for him to speak.

"I told you—it's nothing."

There it was—his walls going up, piece by piece, shutting her out. But Kalista wasn't having it. They had made a promise—honesty, even when it hurt.

She stepped closer until she was right behind him. "You promised you wouldn't do this."

Soren's shoulders stiffened. For a moment, it looked like he might keep stonewalling her. But then he let out a rough sigh, the weight of it dragging him down.

"It's not you, Kali," he muttered, finally turning to face her.

Her heart clenched at the exhaustion etched into his expression—the conflict in his eyes, as if he wanted to let her in but didn't know how.

"Then what is it?" she asked, her voice soft. "Because right now, it feels like you're pulling away."

Soren dragged a hand down his face, frustration flickering in his gaze. "Isabelle was there tonight."

The name hit Kalista like a cold gust of wind. Isabelle. The ex-fiancée. The woman who had shattered Soren's trust and left scars he still carried.

Kalista's stomach twisted, but she kept her voice calm. "What did she want?"

"She's working with Pravus," Soren muttered, bitterness lacing his tone. "They want Drakov Holdings. And she made it clear—if I don't back off, they'll make things ugly."

Kalista narrowed her eyes. "How ugly?"

Soren hesitated, his jaw tightening. "The kind of ugly that winds up in headlines. She's already planting stories, setting the stage. If I don't walk away, the next scandal will be about us."

Kalista's heart skipped, but she kept her expression steady. "You mean me."

Soren's silence was answer enough.

Kalista exhaled slowly, taking in the weight of his silence. She reached out, her hand resting lightly on his arm. "And you're worried I can't handle it."

Soren's jaw tightened. "I know what she's capable of, Kali. I've seen it firsthand. She'll come after you—us—and she won't stop until she's burned everything down."

Kalista tilted her head, a flicker of determination sparking in her eyes. "I knew the risks when I chose this. I'm not scared of her, Ren."

Soren finally looked at her, his gaze heavy with concern. "You should be."

Kalista's hand slid down his arm, her fingers threading through his. "I've dealt with people like Isabelle before. Maybe not at her level, but I've handled worse than threats and rumors."

Soren's grip on her hand tightened, but his gaze remained clouded with doubt.

"Listen to me," Kalista said, her voice steady. "Whatever she tries, we'll face it together. I'm not backing down just because someone's trying to scare us off."

Soren exhaled slowly, his shoulders sagging under the weight of her words. "This isn't just business, Kali. If we keep pushing, she'll make sure it gets personal."

Kalista gave him a small, reassuring smile. "She can try. But I know who I am. And I know who we are. She can't take that from us."

Soren stared at her, his guarded expression softening, the walls around him beginning to crack. "You're too damn calm about this."

Kalista shrugged lightly, her fingers brushing over his knuckles. "That's because I trust us. And I trust you."

The honesty in her words hit him harder than he expected. For a moment, all the tension seemed to drain from his body, replaced by something quieter—something close to relief.

"I don't deserve you," Soren murmured, his voice rough around the edges.

Kalista's smile deepened, warmth flickering in her gaze. "That's not your decision to make."

Soren let out a low, tired chuckle, the sound filled with quiet gratitude. He leaned down, pressing a soft kiss to her forehead, the touch lingering just long enough to steal her breath.

"We'll figure it out," Kalista whispered, her hands resting on his chest.

Soren's arms wrapped around her, pulling her close. "Together."

Chapter 9

Vorlákis Heiress Sets Sights on Ex-Fiancé's Empire Amid Breakup Fallout

The headline glared from Kalista's phone screen, its bold text impossible to ignore. Below, the article painted her as a calculating businesswoman, leveraging her family's empire to dismantle Marius's in a twisted game of corporate revenge. Rumors of infidelity during the relationship, whispers about the timing of the breakup, and sly insinuations about her involvement with Soren Kastellanos made for prime scandal material.

Kalista tossed the phone onto the table, the weight of public scrutiny pressing heavily on her chest. She'd handled her fair share of media nonsense, but this hit closer to home than usual. This time, it wasn't just her reputation at stake—it was the company, her family, and Soren.

The boardroom door swung open, and Soren strode in. His usual cool, composed demeanor was intact, but there was an undercurrent of tension in his every move. He didn't offer any greeting or explanation, only:

"We need to talk."

Kalista leaned back slightly, folding her arms across her chest. "I agree."

Soren dropped into the seat across from her, his gaze hard and unreadable. "That article—"

"I saw it." Kalista cut him off, her voice sharper than she intended. "I figured that's why you've been avoiding me."

Soren exhaled, dragging a hand through his hair. "I wasn't avoiding you."

Kalista's eyes narrowed, frustration bubbling beneath the surface. "Then what would you call it? Because ignoring my texts all day sure felt like avoidance."

Soren's jaw clenched, the muscle flickering along his cheek. "I needed time to think."

Kalista tilted her head, her frustration mounting. "Think about what?"

He looked away, tension radiating from him. "About whether it's smart to keep going like this."

The words struck Kalista like a slap, her stomach twisting painfully. "What exactly are you saying, Ren?"

Soren flinched at the accusation, but instead of denying it, he leaned into the worst possible conclusion. "This thing between us—it's becoming a liability."

Kalista's heart dropped. "A...*liability*?"

Soren's gaze remained fixed on the table. "I'm trying to protect you, Kali. The article is just the start. Isabelle isn't going to stop until she drags both of us through the mud."

Kalista stared at him, disbelief and hurt crashing over her in waves. "So your solution is to cut me off? That's what this is?"

Soren shook his head, frustration clear in every movement. "No. I'm saying—maybe we need to take a step back."

Kalista's chest tightened as his words hit her with full force. "A step back," she echoed, her voice brittle. "You mean walk away."

"I mean, maybe it's for the best." Soren's voice was low, but the damage was already done.

Kalista's breath caught, the weight of his words sinking deep. "You're scared, aren't you? That things will get messy—and I won't be worth the trouble."

Soren flinched, guilt flickering in his gaze. "That's not what I said."

"You didn't have to." Kalista stood abruptly, her palms pressed against the table as she leaned toward him. "You think you're doing the noble thing—keeping me safe by pushing me away. But all you're doing is proving that you don't trust me."

Soren stood too, tension rippling through him. "It's not about trust. It's about avoiding a disaster before it starts."

Kalista's hands trembled, but she forced herself to stay composed. "I thought we were past this. I thought we were in this together."

Soren's jaw tightened, but he couldn't meet her gaze. "I don't know if we can do this, Kali. Not with Isabelle involved."

A sharp pain spread through her chest—anger, betrayal, and disappointment blending into a toxic storm. "So that's it? The second things get hard, you bail?"

Soren looked like he wanted to say something, but no words came.

Kalista's voice broke, quieter now, raw with emotion. "I let you in, Ren. I trusted you. And the moment things start to feel real, you back off and call it a liability."

Soren's silence was louder than any words could have been.

Kalista exhaled slowly, wrapping her arms around herself as if trying to hold together the pieces he'd just shattered. "You promised me honesty. If this isn't about the article or Isabelle, then what is it?"

Soren dragged his hand down his face, looking exhausted. "I don't want to hurt you."

"Too late," Kalista whispered, her voice brittle.

The weight of her words hung heavy in the room, suffocating them both.

"I'm sorry," Soren murmured, his voice rough with regret. "I didn't mean —"

Kalista held up a hand, stopping him. "Don't. If you're going to walk away, just do it. But don't pretend you're doing it for me."

Soren's gaze darkened, guilt and frustration warring in his expression. "Kali…"

"No." Kalista shook her head, forcing a bitter smile. "If you can't trust me enough to stay, then I guess you were right. We can't do this."

For a moment, they stood frozen, the silence between them heavy with everything they couldn't say.

Then, without another word, Soren turned and walked out of the boardroom, leaving Kalista standing there alone, the weight of his departure pressing down on her like a crushing force.

Kalista sat on the couch in her penthouse, a glass of wine in hand, her eyes fixed on the skyline beyond the floor-to-ceiling windows. But the glittering city lights did nothing to ease the ache in her chest.

A sharp knock echoed through the room, and before Kalista could answer, the door swung open. Natalia strolled in, a shopping bag in hand and a concerned look on her face.

"You didn't text me back, so I figured you were either working yourself to death or sulking," Natalia announced, tossing the bag onto the kitchen counter. She gave Kalista a quick once-over, her sharp gaze immediately zeroing in on the wine glass. "Sooo...which one is it?"

Kalista exhaled, rubbing her temple. "Option three. Imploding."

Natalia's playful demeanor shifted. She kicked off her shoes and plopped down next to Kalista on the couch, her tone softening. "Okay, spill. What happened?"

Kalista swirled the wine in her glass, hesitating. But Natalia knew her too well—she wasn't about to let her off the hook.

"Ren and I had a fight," Kalista said quietly, the words tasting bitter on her tongue.

Natalia arched an eyebrow. "A fight? What about?"

"About the article...and Isabelle." Kalista set the wine glass down, her fingers trembling slightly as she spoke. "He thinks this whole thing is going to blow up and hurt me. So his brilliant solution was to...push me away."

Natalia's brows furrowed, sympathy flashing across her face. "He's scared. That's what this is."

"That's what he said," Kalista muttered, pulling her knees to her chest. "But it felt like—like he doesn't trust me. Like the moment things got complicated, he decided I wasn't worth the trouble."

Natalia leaned back, watching her friend carefully. "Do *you* believe that?"

Kalista shook her head, frustration simmering beneath the surface. "I don't know. I told myself we'd take things slow, but...maybe I let myself get too invested. And now...now it just feels like I fell into the same trap all over again."

Natalia reached out, resting a hand on Kalista's shoulder. "This isn't the same as Marius. You left Marius because *he* was the problem. Soren? Soren's different."

"Is he?" Kalista whispered, doubt creeping into her voice. "Because it feels like I keep making the same mistake—trusting people just to watch them pull away."

Natalia gave her a knowing look. "Or maybe...you're scared too. Scared that what you have with Soren is real—and that if it falls apart, it's going to hurt more than anything with Marius ever did."

The words hit Kalista like a punch to the gut. She opened her mouth to argue, but nothing came out. Deep down, she knew Natalia was right. This wasn't like her relationship with Marius—because with Soren, she *cared* in a way that was terrifying.

"Listen," Natalia said gently, giving her shoulder a squeeze. "I know how hard it is to let someone in after being burned. But it's okay to be scared, Kali. That just means it matters."

Kalista ran a hand through her hair, overwhelmed by the realization. "It does matter. And that's what makes it so hard."

Natalia smiled softly, her eyes full of understanding. "You care about him. A lot. And I'm willing to bet he cares about you just as much. But if you both keep letting fear call the shots, you're going to miss out on something real."

Kalista swallowed hard, her heart aching. "What if I've already screwed it up? What if...what if he's done?"

Natalia shook her head. "He's not done. Trust me. Soren is an idiot, but he's your idiot. And if you want this, Kali—if you really want it—then you've got to fight for it."

Kalista pressed her lips together, her mind racing. She hated how vulnerable this made her feel—how exposed. But Natalia was right. Walking away from this, from Soren, wasn't what she wanted. What scared her wasn't that things had gotten complicated—it was how much she wanted them to work.

After a long moment, Kalista whispered, "What if I try...and it still falls apart?"

Natalia gave her a soft smile, her hand still resting on her shoulder. "Then at least you'll know you gave it everything. But I don't think it's going to fall apart, Kali. I think it's going to be messy and imperfect, but I think it's worth it."

Kalista exhaled slowly, the knot in her chest loosening just a little. Maybe Natalia was right. Maybe this wasn't about avoiding the risk—it was about deciding whether Soren was worth it. And the answer, as terrifying as it was, felt crystal clear.

He was.

The office door swung open without a knock, and Lysander strolled in, casual as always, with that infuriating smirk tugging at the corner of his mouth.

"You're brooding," Lysander announced as he leaned against the edge of the desk, crossing his arms. "It's a bad look for you."

Soren didn't glance up. "I'm not in the mood, Lys."

"You're never in the mood," Lysander quipped, though there was a trace of concern beneath the teasing. He nudged the whiskey glass with two fingers. "So, are we drinking to celebrate, or commiserate?"

Soren let out a low sigh, running a hand through his hair. "I messed up."

Lysander gave a small, knowing hum. "Let me guess—Kalista?"

Soren's silence was answer enough.

Lysander arched a brow, his smirk softening. "What'd you do?"

Soren exhaled sharply, frustration lacing his voice. "I told myself I was protecting her. But all I did was push her away."

Lysander nodded slowly, as if this confirmed everything he already suspected. "And now you're sitting here, drinking alone, pretending you don't care."

"I do care," Soren muttered, almost to himself. "More than I thought I would."

"That's the problem, isn't it?" Lysander said with a small grin. "You're not used to caring. Makes you feel...exposed."

Soren shot him a dark look. "Thanks for the insight, Dr. Phil."

Lysander chuckled but didn't push further. "Look, I know you, Ren. You don't do things halfway. You either go all in, or you don't bother. And right now, you're acting like you've already lost."

Soren leaned back in his chair, dragging a hand down his face. "What if I have?"

Lysander tilted his head, studying him for a moment. "Do you want to lose her?"

The question hit Soren harder than he expected. He sat in silence, the weight of it pressing down on him. Did he want to lose Kalista? The thought of her slipping away—of her walking out of his life—made his chest tighten painfully.

"No," Soren admitted quietly. "I don't want to lose her."

Lysander smiled, though there was genuine warmth in his expression. "Then stop acting like you already have."

Soren shook his head, frustration gnawing at him. "It's not that simple. I've spent years keeping people out, Lys. I don't know how to...do this. How to be with someone like her."

Lysander's smile softened. "That's the thing, Ren. You don't have to have it all figured out. You just have to *try*. And maybe stop treating her like one of your acquisitions."

Soren let out a low chuckle despite himself, though the weight on his chest didn't lift. "Easier said than done."

"Look, man," Lysander said, his tone shifting to something more serious. "If she means something to you—and it sounds like she does—you've got to stop running from it. You've already spent half your life building walls. Maybe it's time you let someone through."

Soren stared down at the glass in his hand, the whiskey swirling lazily inside. He knew Lysander was right. He had spent so long guarding himself from pain, from loss, that he had forgotten how to let anyone get close. But Kalista had slipped through those cracks—whether he wanted her to or not. And he didn't want to push her away. Not anymore.

Soren set the glass down with a quiet clink, the decision settling in his chest.

"I want this," he said aloud, more to himself than to Lysander. "I want her."

Lysander gave a satisfied nod, clapping a hand on Soren's shoulder. "Then go get her, idiot."

Soren shot him a dry look. "You have a real gift for motivational speeches."

Lysander grinned. "That's what friends are for."

Chapter 10

The text had come late in the afternoon, just as Kalista was finishing a meeting at Vorlákis Enterprises.

Ren

Meet me on the rooftop garden tonight? 7 p.m.?

There was no explanation, no preamble. Just a time and a place. But Kalista knew exactly which rooftop garden he meant—the quiet one hidden above the city, where string lights draped lazily over ivy-covered trellises, and the hum of the world below faded into a distant murmur. It was one of her favorite places to escape when the demands of the business—or life— became too much.

She had mentioned it in passing to Soren weeks ago. She hadn't expected him to remember, let alone invite her there now. And yet, as she stepped through the rooftop entrance, the warm glow of the garden lights and the soft scent of jasmine made it feel like the world had paused, just for them.

Soren stood at the edge of the garden, hands in his pockets, staring out at the city skyline. He turned when he heard her approach, his expression a mixture of hope and uncertainty. He looked as impeccable as always in his dark tailored suit, but there was something different tonight—something vulnerable in the way he held himself, as if he wasn't sure how this moment would go.

"Kali." Her name on his lips was soft, like a plea.

She paused a few steps away from him, her arms crossed loosely. "What is this, Ren?"

His gaze searched hers, as if gathering the courage to say what had been weighing on him. "You mentioned this place once. Said it was where you come to clear your head when everything feels too heavy." He gave a small, self-conscious shrug. "I figured...maybe it's where we need to talk."

Kalista's brow furrowed, her heart already twisting with a mix of anticipation and uncertainty. "Why now? Why tonight?"

Soren took a slow, steady breath. "Because I needed to say something. And I didn't want to mess it up again."

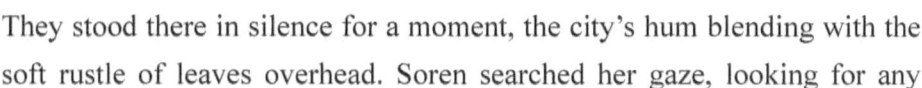

They stood there in silence for a moment, the city's hum blending with the soft rustle of leaves overhead. Soren searched her gaze, looking for any sign that she was willing to hear him out.

"I've spent most of my life keeping people at arm's length," he began, his voice low and deliberate. "It's how I stay in control. I thought if I kept things manageable between us, I wouldn't have to risk losing you."

Kalista's chest tightened, but she stayed quiet, waiting for him to continue.

"I convinced myself I was protecting you by pulling back," Soren admitted. "But the truth is, I was protecting myself. I was scared—scared of what it would mean to let you in, scared of what would happen if I lost you." His voice softened, filled with raw honesty. "But you've shown me that life doesn't fit into neat little boxes. That love and work, business and personal —they don't have to be at odds."

He took a small step closer, his gaze steady. "You're worth every risk, Kali. You're worth everything."

Her heart swelled at his words, but fear still lingered at the edges. It wasn't just him who had been afraid—she had been too.

"I was scared too," she whispered, her voice trembling slightly. "Not of being with you, but of what stepping into the business would mean for me. I thought...if I took on this role, I'd have to give up my dream of being creative, of doing what I love."

Soren's expression softened, and he reached for her hand, threading his fingers gently through hers. "You don't have to give anything up, Kali. You can be both. You are both."

She squeezed his hand, her throat tightening. "That's what you've shown me, Ren. You've made me see that I don't have to choose between being creative and running the company. I can do it all...and I want to do it with you."

Soren's gaze darkened, a flicker of emotion passing through his eyes. "You don't have to do any of it alone. I'll be with you. Every step of the way."

Kalista felt her heart break open, all the fear, doubt, and hesitation melting away. For the first time, she wasn't just stepping into her future—she was embracing it, fully and without reservation.

"I love you, Ren," she whispered, the words spilling from her without hesitation. "I don't know when it happened, but I do. I love you."

Soren's breath caught, his grip on her hand tightening. "I love you too, Kali. More than I ever thought I could."

They stood there for a beat longer, the weight of their words settling between them, thick with meaning. And then Soren pulled her into his arms, capturing her lips in a kiss that was both fierce and tender.

The world beyond the garden fell away, leaving only the two of them beneath the soft glow of the lights.

When they finally broke apart, Soren rested his forehead against hers, his hands still cradling her face. "We'll figure it out," he whispered, his voice rough with emotion.

Kalista smiled, her heart full and steady. "Together."

Kalista took her seat at the head of the table, glancing briefly at Soren, who gave her a small, encouraging nod. It was a simple gesture, but it carried the weight of everything they had promised each other the night before.

Her heart felt lighter—steady, grounded in a way she hadn't experienced in years. She let the calm settle over her, embracing the moment as the boardroom filled with quiet murmurs. But there was still one thing left to address. One final piece of business Isabelle had tried to weaponize.

"Before we begin," Kalista said, her voice clear and deliberate, "I want to address the article circulating about my engagement to Marius Drakov."

The room fell silent, every gaze locking onto her. She could feel the tension ripple through the air—people who had undoubtedly read the piece, waiting to see how she would respond. Soren leaned back in his chair, his expression composed, though his eyes were steady on her, a quiet reassurance she didn't know she needed.

Kalista clasped her hands on the table, her gaze sweeping over the board members. "I want to be clear—this acquisition is not personal. The failure of my engagement has no bearing on the strategic decisions we're making as a company."

A few murmurs stirred, but she held up a hand, her voice unwavering. "Marius made his choices, both personally and professionally, and I made mine. This acquisition is about seizing an opportunity that benefits Vorlákis Enterprises—nothing more. I won't allow tabloid gossip to dictate how we run this company."

The confidence in her voice silenced any lingering doubts. She wasn't pleading her case—she was setting the terms. It was a shift the board hadn't expected, and Kalista could feel their respect for her deepening in the stillness that followed.

She glanced toward Mr. Livanos, one of the most senior members of the board and a man who had expressed concerns about the negative press. His expression softened as he gave a slow, approving nod.

"We appreciate your clarity, Ms. Vorlákis," Livanos said, his tone measured but approving. "The board is aligned with your strategy."

Kalista allowed herself a small breath of relief. But she wasn't finished.

"And," she continued, her voice steady, "I also want to address the insinuations about my relationship with Mr. Kastellanos."

This time, the murmurs grew louder—shocked, curious, intrigued. But Kalista met the board's collective gaze head-on, unwavering.

"I've worked closely with Mr. Kastellanos because our partnership benefits both our companies. Any personal relationship we have beyond that is not for public consumption, nor does it impact the integrity of our work together."

Soren's lips curved slightly, just enough to suggest amusement, though his eyes were filled with pride. He hadn't expected her to tackle it so directly —but this was Kalista, after all.

"I understand that rumors are unavoidable," Kalista said, her tone calm but firm. "But I won't allow them to undermine the work we've done or the decisions we've made. My personal life is just that—personal. What matters here is that this acquisition will strengthen Vorlákis Enterprises and set us up for long-term success."

The murmurs faded into silence, and one by one, the board members exchanged looks of agreement.

"We stand by your leadership, Ms. Vorlákis," Livanos said, his voice carrying the finality Kalista needed to hear.

With a nod of approval from the rest of the table, the weight of Isabelle's attempted sabotage lifted from her shoulders. Kalista allowed herself a small, triumphant smile.

She glanced at Soren, who gave her an almost imperceptible nod—a gesture that said everything she needed to know: You've got this.

"Let's move forward," Kalista said, her voice steady and assured. "The Drakov acquisition isn't going to finalize itself."

The meeting resumed, conversations shifting back to strategy, projections, and timelines. But even as she focused on the details, a quiet sense of peace settled within her.

She had faced the worst—the gossip, the doubts, even her own fears—and had come out stronger. She hadn't just defended herself; she had claimed her place at the table, fully and unapologetically.

And as the meeting pressed on, she knew without a doubt that whatever challenges came next, she wouldn't be facing them alone.

After the meeting, as the board members dispersed and the room began to empty, Soren lingered by her side. He leaned close, just enough that only she could hear him.

"You handled that perfectly," he murmured, his voice warm with admiration.

Kalista smiled, a soft, genuine smile that reached her eyes. "Told you I could handle it."

Soren's eyes sparkled with a mix of pride and affection. "I never doubted it for a second."

Epilogue

Talia

> Just previewed your collection. It's stunning, Kali.
> You're going to make waves.

Kalista smiled down at her phone, the weight of Natalia's words settling warmly in her chest. Natalia had been with her through everything—every mistake, every triumph, and every moment in between. Now, with the launch of her first collection under her leadership only days away, Natalia's message felt like a quiet reminder of how far she had come.

She set her phone down and looked out over the city from the window of her office. The skyline stretched before her, bathed in the soft glow of the setting sun. Her desk was a reflection of who she had become—sketches of bold designs layered alongside business reports. Creativity and strategy, woven together seamlessly.

For years, she'd feared that stepping into the business side of things would mean giving up the creative part of herself. But now, as she glanced over a gown design laid out across her desk, she felt nothing but peace. This collection was hers—every stitch, every decision, every piece of it reflected both her vision and the leadership she'd grown into.

A framed photo caught her eye—a candid shot of her and Soren, laughing together at home. She smiled softly. Soren had been there through every step of this journey, nudging her to see that she didn't have to choose between her passion and her role in the family business. She could do both. And she wasn't doing any of it alone.

A knock on the door pulled her from her thoughts, and her assistant stepped inside with a bright smile. "Ms. Vorlákis, the board is ready for your final presentation before the launch."

Kalista nodded, gathering her notes with steady hands. "Let's do this."

Across town, Soren sat at his desk in Kastellanos Ventures, the afternoon light casting shadows over stacks of papers. Yet his focus was elsewhere—on a small box in his hand, the weight of it far heavier than its size.

He turned the box over slowly, the black velvet smooth beneath his fingers. Inside was a ring—simple but elegant, just like the woman he had fallen for.

His phone buzzed, pulling him from his thoughts. A message from Kalista appeared on the screen.

Kali

Final meeting before the launch. Wish me luck.

Soren's lips curled into a soft smile, his heart warming as he typed his reply.

Ren

You don't need luck. You've got this.

As soon as he set the phone down, the door swung open, and Lysander strolled in, hands in his pockets and that familiar smirk tugging at the corner of his mouth.

"You're smiling," Lysander said, leaning casually against the desk. "That's new. Should I be concerned?"

Soren chuckled, shaking his head. "Don't get used to it."

Lysander raised an eyebrow, catching the small black box before Soren could slip it out of sight. "What do we have here?"

Soren hesitated for only a moment, then opened the box, revealing the ring. "Thinking of a new joint venture."

Lysander blinked, genuinely surprised for once. "Well, damn. Didn't think I'd see the day."

Soren leaned back in his chair, running a hand through his hair. "She's...changed things for me. This isn't just about building something on my own anymore. I want to build something with her."

Lysander gave a low whistle, folding his arms over his chest. "That's a hell of a venture. Risky."

Soren's smile deepened, his eyes steady. "Yeah, but it's the only one that matters."

For a moment, Lysander just watched him, the sarcasm slipping from his expression, replaced by something almost like pride. "You've got it bad, Kastellanos. But...this might actually suit you."

Soren chuckled, snapping the ring box shut and tucking it into his pocket. "That's the plan."

Lysander clapped a hand on Soren's shoulder, his grin returning. "Well, good luck with that. And if she says no...well, I'll be here to say 'I told you so.'"

Soren shook his head with a quiet laugh. "She won't."

Lysander grinned. "That's the spirit."

As Lysander turned to leave, Soren leaned back in his chair, the weight of the ring now feeling lighter in his pocket. He knew exactly what he wanted —and for the first time in a long time, he wasn't afraid to go after it.

The outdoor fashion show had been nothing short of breathtaking. Under a starlit sky, Kalista's collection had shimmered on the runway, each piece a celebration of who she had become—creative, bold, and fearless. As applause erupted around her, she stepped out for her bow, the warmth of the crowd wrapping around her like the finest silk.

But it wasn't the ovation that made her heart skip. It was the man standing at the back of the crowd, hands in his pockets, his dark eyes steady and filled with quiet pride.

Soren.

As the applause began to fade and guests mingled, Kalista made her way through the throng until she reached him. The noise around them dulled, leaving only the two of them in their own little world.

"You were incredible," Soren said softly, his gaze never leaving hers.

Kalista smiled, brushing a strand of hair behind her ear. "I couldn't have done it without you."

Soren shook his head, taking her hand in his. "You did this, Kali. You've built something amazing."

Her heart swelled, emotion catching in her throat. "We both have."

Soren squeezed her hand gently. "Actually...I was hoping we could build something else together."

Kalista blinked, a flicker of confusion in her eyes. "What do you mean?"

Soren gave her hand one last squeeze before reaching into his pocket. Her breath caught when he pulled out a small velvet box.

"I've been thinking," Soren began, his voice low and steady, though there was a flicker of nerves beneath it. "You and me...we've done a lot of deals, worked on a lot of ventures. But this one? This is the only one that really matters."

He opened the box, revealing the ring inside—a perfect blend of elegance and simplicity.

"Kalista Vorlákis," Soren said, his voice full of warmth and certainty, "will you be my partner? In life, in love, and in everything else? Will you marry me?"

Kalista's breath hitched, her heart racing as tears welled in her eyes. She stared at him—this man who had challenged her, believed in her, and stood by her through it all.

A slow, radiant smile spread across her face. "I thought you'd never ask."

Soren's lips twitched into a grin, relief and joy flooding his features. "So...is that a yes?"

Kalista laughed, brushing away a tear as she nodded. "Yes, Ren. A thousand times yes."

Soren slipped the ring onto her finger, the gesture both simple and profound. And then, before the crowd and the city lights, he pulled her into his arms and kissed her—a kiss that felt like the beginning of forever.

The world around them faded once more, leaving only the two of them, entwined in a love that was stronger than any business venture, deeper than any partnership. They had taken risks, faced fears, and fought for what they had—and now, they were exactly where they were meant to be.

When they finally pulled apart, Kalista rested her forehead against his, her heart full.

"So," she whispered, her eyes twinkling with joy, "what's next for us, Mr. Kastellanos?"

Soren smiled, his thumb brushing over her cheek. "Whatever we want, Mrs. Kastellanos."